PENGUIN BOOKS

# THE DISCREET PLEASURES OF REJECTION

MARTIN PAGE was born in 1975. In college he was a dilettante student, studying law, psychology, linguistics, philosophy, sociology, art history, and anthropology at different points. His novels have been translated into a dozen languages, and he's also written prefaces for the French translations of Oscar Wilde's *The Soul of Man under Socialism* and *Pen, Pencil and Poison*, Horst Hamann's *Paris Vertical*, and Balzac's *Traité des excitants modernes*, a postscript to Brillat-Savarin's *The Physiology of Taste*. He lives in Paris.

BRUCE BENDERSON has translated works by Alain Robbe-Grillet, Philippe Sollers, Pierre Guyotat, Grégoire Bouillier, Tony Duvert, Virginie Despentes, Nelly Arcan, and others. He is also the author of *The Romanian: Story of an Obsession*, a memoir that won France's Prix de Flore in its French translation, and the novels *User* and *Pacific Agony*. As a journalist, Benderson has written for *The New York Times Magazine*, *The Village Voice*, *Vogue*, *Madame Figaro*, and many other publications.

Also by Martin Page
HOW I BECAME STUPID

# THE DISCREET PLEASURES OF REJECTION

## MARTIN PAGE

Translated by
BRUCE BENDERSON

PENGUIN BOOKS

PENGUIN BOOKS

Published by the Penguin Group

Penguin Group (USA) Inc., 375 Hudson Street, New York, New York 10014, U.S.A.
Penguin Group (Canada), 90 Eglinton Avenue East, Suite 700, Toronto, Ontario, Canada
M4P 2Y3 (a division of Pearson Penguin Canada Inc.)
Penguin Books Ltd, 80 Strand, London WC2R 0RL, England
Penguin Ireland, 25 St Stephen's Green, Dublin 2, Ireland
(a division of Penguin Books Ltd)
Penguin Group (Australia), 250 Camberwell Road, Camberwell, Victoria 3124, Australia
(a division of Pearson Australia Group Pty Ltd)
Penguin Books India Pvt Ltd, 11 Community Centre, Panchsheel Park,
New Delhi–110 017, India
Penguin Group (NZ), 67 Apollo Drive, Rosedale, North Shore 0632, New Zealand
(a division of Pearson New Zealand Ltd)
Penguin Books (South Africa) (Pty) Ltd, 24 Sturdee Avenue, Rosebank,
Johannesburg 2196, South Africa

Penguin Books Ltd, Registered Offices:
80 Strand, London WC2R 0RL, England

First published in Penguin Books 2010

1 3 5 7 9 10 8 6 4 2

Originally published in French as *Peut-etre une histoire d'amour* by Editions de
l'Olivier, Paris. Copyright © Editions de l'Olivier, 2008.

PUBLISHER'S NOTE
This is a work of fiction. Names, characters, places, and incidents either are the product of
the author's imagination or are used fictitiously, and any resemblance to actual persons,
living or dead, business establishments, events, or locales is entirely coincidental.

LIBRARY OF CONGRESS CATALOGING IN PUBLICATION DATA
Page, Martin, 1975–
[Peut-être une histoire d'amour. English]
The discreet pleasures of rejection / Martin Page ; translated by Bruce Benderson.
p. cm.
"Originally published in French as Peut-être une histoire d'amour by Editions de
l'Olivier, Paris . . . 2008."—T.p. verso.
ISBN 978-0-14-311652-3
I. Benderson, Bruce. II. Title.
PQ2716.A35P4813 2010
843'.92—dc22    2009034105

Printed in the United States of America
Set in Old Style 7 • Designed by Sabrina Bowers

# Acknowledgments

I thank Alix and Laurent.

I learned of the death of Jean-Pierre Vernant during the writing of this novel. I'd like to take the opportunity here to say how much the man and the scholar, the Resistance fighter and the anthropologist means to me. He is a model for anyone who values Greek antiquity, the stories that people invent and tell about themselves, and political struggle. This book is dedicated to him. Much too infrequently, the writer of fiction, happily starving and eternally dabbling in learning, pays homage to his invisible masters, teachers who, without being aware of it, contribute daily to the enrichment of his imagination and to the expression of his obsessions. I could cover several pages with the names of such strangely familiar people to whom I'd like to express my gratitude. In the present context, I'd especially like to thank Pierre Hadot for his books.

A special thank you to Amalia Tarallo for her kindness and for the welcome she gave me in São Paulo.

# THE DISCREET PLEASURES OF REJECTION

Virgil's shoes slapped the wet street. He'd left Svengali Communications later than usual. Just as the sun was setting he'd noticed the face of the clock above the door.

Located between the Louvre, the Council of State, and the Comédie-Française, the offices of the advertising agency where Virgil worked were in fine company. The entrance to the subway station, caked with multicolored pearls like a child's creation for Mother's Day, appealed to him. Even so, Virgil and this part of the city weren't exactly at home with each other; rubbing shoulders, they kept on their guard, both realizing that things could end badly. The young man claimed only two little islands in this gilded section of the first arrondissement: the Libraire Delamain and the restaurant-café called Á Jean Nicot, the only dive left that wasn't overrun by the smart set. He got onto the bus and punched his ticket. Six months ago he'd stopped taking the subway, weary as he was of putting up with a constant feeling of suffocation, spiked with moments of pure panic.

His body followed the meanderings of his mind. He'd

leave the workday little by little. He couldn't handle just walking out of the office, taking the elevator, and going through the doors of the building. He needed a transition. The race through traffic, the movement of the bus's wheels as well as his eyes, which focused on pedestrians, cars, and bicycles, got rid of that day's work and his co-workers. As he got closer to home, he'd find himself again. He wasn't always his best company, but the coexistence of what he thought he was, what he wanted to be, and what he was occurred without much argument.

After nearly knocking down a homeless person, the bus stopped in front of the Gare du Nord. Armelle wasn't at her usual table outside the Terminus. Virgil would have liked to catch a glimpse of her, a touch of lipstick on her mouth, holding a book. He'd get together with her after dinner for a drink.

He said hello to two prostitutes in front of his building. They smiled at him and waved. His mailbox was empty. He climbed the stairs two at a time to the fourth floor, opened the door to his apartment, and tossed the keys into the fruit basket with the bananas and apples.

The red LED on his old cassette answering machine was blinking. Virgil liked getting messages; whether they were from friends or people selling full-service kitchens, they reminded him that he existed in society. But the very first thing he had to do was make something to chow down on, so he inspected the fridge: eggs, some leftover tomatoes wilting in a can, an impressive collection of yogurts. He broke two eggs over a frying pan, covered them, and finally went to push the PLAY button on the machine.

"Virgil," said a woman's voice.

He got closer to the speaker to get a better dose of the captivating voice. God had a woman's voice, he figured. The message went on:

"It's Clara. I'm sorry, but I'd rather stop here. I'm leaving you, Virgil. I'm leaving you."

He listened to the message five more times. The eggs were burning in the frying pan. He splashed cold water on his face, looked at himself in the mirror of the medicine cabinet. He closed his eyes, then opened them after a few seconds. He swallowed a tranquilizer, and went back to the kitchen and turned off the gas. The eggs looked like two pieces of coal, and the smoke coming off them was pungent.

No experience is as painful as a breakup. The separation feels like a meticulously planned assault—because the bomb is placed inside your heart, there's no escaping the violence of the explosion. In the current case, however, Virgil was learning that he'd been dumped by a woman he didn't know and, it was patently obvious, with whom he'd never been. At the same time that he reeled from the shock of discovering he was the object of rejected love, he was aware that the situation lacked reality.

In Virgil's eyes, Earth had never been a very stable heavenly body. He hung on to what little there was that was certain. He was a bachelor. Of course. He had a bachelor's fridge, habits. You could count more on his being single than you could on gravity.

He focused on the things in the room that he found reassuring: his vinyl collection, the red and yellow poster for his parents' circus above the couch with the sagging armrests, the can of chicory coffee, a telephone bill stuck to the fridge with a magnet shaped like an African elephant (its big triangular ears open like the wings of a butterfly, its trunk raised between its tusks). He unplugged the answering machine and left the apartment.

Concentrating on his steps, he walked down the boulevard de Magenta. His body functioned, his joints and muscles were still okay, the blood was flowing in his veins. On the other hand, his brain was close to overheating.

The big, black, sharp-edged telephone answering machine stayed pinned against his chest during the trip to the passage des Petites-Écuries, where his psychoanalyst's office was located. The only thing this neighborhood had in common with the one surrounding Virgil's office was the large number of covered passageways that let you avoid the busy street. The people who lived in the Petites-Écuries alleyway had put out some chairs and a white garden table, a couple of retirees were tending some rosebushes, a child's bicycle had been left outside. Dr. Zetkin's lair was perched on the fourth floor of the building, in a corner of the courtyard. The vertical and horizontal beams and crossbeams poked through the façade, forming a web of thick brown strands. At the top you could make out gargoyles that kept the rainwater from soaking the wood and the plaster.

In the waiting room, a young woman (wearing wool pants and a black jacket, her hair in a ponytail), the last patient of the day, was leafing through a magazine. Seeing Virgil with a telephone answering machine pressed against his heart seemed to disturb her. She stared down at her reading material. The door of the office opened; Dr. Zetkin's hand appeared and signaled the young woman inside.

Virgil hummed the last jingle he'd heard at the agency. The notes of that ad, bragging about the health benefits of applesauce, calmed him. Normally he'd go over his anxieties of the moment, list the subjects to tackle, construct an infallible way of talking about them, and prepare some counterarguments to Dr. Zetkin's probable challenges. But this time he preferred not to use his brain. After twenty minutes, the young woman came out.

Dr. Zetkin was a woman of about fifty, with salt-and-pepper hair and green horn-rimmed glasses; she was wearing a violet cardigan of soft wool over a cream-colored blouse, a pearl necklace, and some jade and amber rings. Her office was filled with the odor of Lapsang souchong tea. Virgil thought it tasted too strong, but there was a moment during a session when its odor alone produced an immediate sense of well-being.

"Hello, Doctor."

"You didn't have an appointment."

She gestured to Virgil to enter. They sat down at opposite ends of the room. A red cast-iron teapot was steaming on a sideboard near the library. The big appointment book with the black cover open in front of the doctor looked like a bird of prey in flight. The page for that day was filled with names that didn't include Virgil's—Monday wasn't his day.

Virgil had gone beyond the transference stage, so he wasn't jealous of Dr. Zetkin's other clients. In fact, he assumed that her many patients helped her to see that he was more interesting than the pack of ordinary neurotics. The relationship you have with a shrink can't get out of hand—if the person is a genuine professional, he or she won't accept invitations to exhibitions you send. Shrinks don't become friends, or enemies. Purely speaking, they're not human. "Give me a fulcrum and I'll lift the world," said Archimedes, challenging his friends from Syracuse. In this instance, Virgil had to rise above his neuroses. His psychoanalyst was the only stable element in his universe; she played the role of fulcrum.

"I just had an accident," said Virgil.

"Oh. What kind?"

"An accident with reality."

More than muggings, illnesses, or car accidents, reality is the major dealer of wounds, injuries, suffering. Virgil placed the answering machine on the desk. Dr. Zetkin squinted and crossed her arms. Virgil didn't respect the rules. He should have been lying on the couch, not sitting. Not ruining the geography of her office. He knew that Dr. Zetkin saw his behavior as a symptom. It wasn't something he could hold against her, because he himself was always saying that any human action at all (for example, breathing) was a symptom.

"Ah," she said.

As usual, her face revealed nothing. Virgil managed to detect the nuances in her blank expressions. There was curious neutrality, cold neutrality, and reassuring neutrality. What's more, Dr. Zetkin had an impressive talent for saying "ah." It was the foundation of her entire vocabulary. From time to time she used other words, such as "well," "meaning what?" "yes," or "you forgot to pay me." The woman survived in society and excelled in her field with a dozen expressions that she used stingily.

After pulling out the cord of the lamp on the desk to plug in the answering machine, Virgil pushed the button. The message began to play.

"So, this woman broke up with you," said the psychoanalyst.

"Not exactly."

"She's awfully clear about it. You won't accept it."

Dr. Zetkin thought she'd put her finger on the problem. After all, they both knew what Virgil's love life was like; his being dumped certainly was plausible. It was in the natural order of things, like tides or the migration of wild geese. Virgil was almost happy about going against the grain of it and, for once, doing such a thing made sense.

"We weren't together. I don't even know her."

Dr. Zetkin picked up her glasses and began to clean the lenses. The case interested her. After a day of listening to classic neuroses, she wasn't averse to a bit of fantasy. She put her glasses back on and widened the space between her hands in a gesture of interrogation.

"Then, how do you interpret this?"

"I don't want to interpret, I want to understand."

"Ah, really?"

This environment felt secure to Virgil. The major works of psychoanalysis filled the bookshelves, a photo of Freud pointing through the window of a train arriving in Paris in 1938 hung behind the desk, a framed copy of the first manuscript page of his study on Jensen's *Gravida* was on another wall, specialists' journals in French and Spanish were scattered on the desk. Virgil liked to think that animistic spirits inside the relics turned the place into a kind of sanctuary. He could pull the lid off his brain without being afraid.

"It can't be a mistake," he said. "She mentions my first name."

Virgil didn't have a common first name, as he'd discovered early on, on the playground.

"Maybe it's a joke," he went on.

"And why would a woman who doesn't know you want to play a practical joke on you?"

Virgil's cell phone rang. He'd been too preoccupied with what was happening to remember to turn it off. Given the point of disrespect for the rules of analysis that he'd reached, he answered it. It was Faustine, his old girlfriend.

"Faustine, I can't talk, I'm at my shrink's. What? I'll call you back."

He hung up. Things weren't going well. He stared at the photograph of Freud. His hands were sweating, his ears felt blocked, his saliva tasted like iron. He was having trouble catching his breath. It was like he was involved in an accident, the victim of a pileup with an invisible force.

"Did I tell you about Faustine already?"

"She's one of the women you fell in love with who's now a friend."

Virgil didn't know why, but in order to become friends with a woman, he had to fall in love with her first.

"She just found out that Clara left me. She was offering to take me to dinner, to comfort me."

"Think. You're sure you never met a *Clara*?"

With half-closed eyes, the doctor studied Virgil. Had the delicate border between reality and fiction been ruptured? Virgil concentrated on a breathing exercise he'd picked up in yoga class.

A memory surfaced. From a month ago, during an evening at Maud's. Every weekend she used her parents' immense apartment to throw a party whose main feature was the noise level, which kept you from hearing the banalities being exchanged by too many guests. Virgil had been drinking. Faustine yanked him by the sleeve and tried to introduce a girl to him. He pictured his friend saying her name as she jiggled her oversize cocktail: Clara. But Virgil couldn't remember her face or their conversation. Anyway, nothing had happened. Virgil described the episode to Dr. Zetkin.

"Maybe you kissed her and she misinterpreted the gesture?"

"I shake women's hands. Especially when I've been drinking. If not, my lips tend to slide all over their face. Could I have had an affair with her without being aware of it?"

"You're not crazy."

The statement rattled Virgil. All of a sudden, without any lead-up, his psychoanalyst, who'd been seeing him three times a week for five years, was tearing him away from one of his anxieties.

"You're not just saying that to reassure me?"

"You pay me for my objectivity."

Virgil's telephone rang again. It was Nadia. The conversation was brief. Faustine had told her about the breakup. A beep signaled a call waiting. He put Nadia on hold. It was Faustine again. He promised his friends that he'd call them back. Dr. Zetkin took notes.

"I don't feel very well," said Virgil after turning off his phone.

He wanted to throw up and pass out at the same time. Something was wrong, and he didn't know what it was. He had a feeling it was serious and that his life would be radically changed by it.

"Get some rest."

"That isn't going to solve anything."

"Everything doesn't get solved."

There was no hurry. Dr. Zetkin suspected that time would shed some light on things. Virgil was waiting to see what would happen as well, but he was no spectator. The psychoanalyst tapped the edge of the desk with her pen.

"I don't know if this has anything to do with it," Virgil proposed, "but I've been getting dizzy spells lately. And nausea."

He needed to find some meaning for what was happening. Illness always provided a special refuge for him when he felt overwhelmed.

"You really think you're sick?"

"I'm trying to understand what's going on."

"Think so?"

Virgil felt as if his blood had frozen in his veins. There were bright spots swimming in his eyes.

"Just as a precaution," he said, having trouble swallowing, "you could prescribe a few tests for me."

"If that's what you want."

The doctor wrote enough words on a prescription for them not to look like *a few tests*. Among his talents, Virgil possessed the rare faculty of being able to read the word *scan* upside down.

"A CAT scan?" exclaimed Virgil.

"Don't worry."

"Don't worry" has to be the most alarming phrase in the entire French language. Virgil glanced out the window. The passage des Petites-Écuries had been plunged into darkness. He didn't feel like leaving, wanted to stay in this room and wrap himself into the plaid design of the couch. Dr. Zetkin opened the door. Virgil walked out with his arms pressed against his sides. He took the streets that were the best lit and the busiest; he walked past the fast-food places on the rue du Faubourg-Saint-Denis, to take advantage of the light coming from shops and the fried-food smells from the kebab vendors. The slightest sign of life was precious to him.

He had to make a series of telephone calls to Dr. Zetkin's medical connections in order to get an appointment at a radiology office for the following day.

There was no doubt about the outcome. A woman had left him, and he had no memory of their being together, so he was suffering from a neurological disease. The area having to do with memory had been affected; entire sections of his existence were disappearing with the onset of the illness. When he concentrated, he thought he could hear the devastation advancing. Of course, medicine had made considerable progress in recent years. But he wasn't the type to fool himself with false illusions.

I'm going to die, thought Virgil. He repeated the sentence aloud several times. The end was near, he was sure of it. A shiver traveled from head to toe. He feared death, not because he wouldn't be around anymore—he was used to the feeling of not being in the world—but because dying meant becoming normal. A corpse has no personality. It wasn't an instinct for preservation in Virgil that made death seem unbearable, it was his spirit of contradiction.

He turned the light down and sat on the couch. His fingers searched the fabric for bumps, defects, worn-out areas, the circle of a cigarette burn. Desperate for sensations and for data, he palpated the objects around him like Helen Keller skimming a book in Braille. He had lived in this apartment for seven years. He'd left his impression on it the way a foot gives its particular shape to a shoe. Could you say the same thing about the world? When we die, does the world's matter retain our imprint? Do the atoms conserve the contours of our thoughts? At least, thought Virgil, the apartment would continue to exist, his friends would keep living, his books and records would be adopted by others.

For dinner, he ignored the cost. On Bon Marché's Internet site he ordered a feast and three bottles of wine. The basket was delivered in half an hour. To a small extent, the quality of the meal overpowered his somber reflections. He listened to his favorite vinyls. Performers from all over the world and every period succeeded one another in his living room: a last concert in his honor.

Carrying a glass of wine, he strolled through his two rooms, wanting to touch every square inch of them and leave behind his fingerprints. The deltas, ridges, curves, curls, and whorls of the fleshy part of his fingers would fossilize. No cleaning, no demolition would erase the proofs of his existence. These traces would stay hiding in

the obscurity of the infinitely small, waiting for archae-
ologists to discover them. He'd seen an article on the
potters of antiquity who, modeling the clay on their
wheel, unknowingly cut—as if on a record—the words
pronounced during their work. His apartment was covered with millions of grooves from his monologues and
conversations.

Despite his efforts, Virgil could not manage to remember Clara. He went through his life after last month's
party: hanging out with Armelle at the Terminus Nord
in the late evening, telephone calls to his parents, the
female neighbor who'd loaned him a condom, his work
at the agency, the times he went out, the movies he'd seen,
the books he'd read. On a sheet of paper he reconstructed
the better part of each day. But no Clara reappeared. The
disease had eliminated her.

During the second bottle of wine, overcome by the
alcohol, he imagined the comings and goings of this mys-
terious woman. He saw her placing a hand on the door-
frame of the kitchen, opening the fridge and pouring
herself a glass of soy milk, coming out of the shower with
a towel knotted above her breasts. He searched for vestiges of her presence; he looked under the bed, emptied
the closets, inspected the medicine cabinet. But he found
no earring, no stocking, no strand of long hair, no tube of
moisturizing cream. Because noise traveled into the

neighboring apartments, he waited a certain period of time before inviting any girl to his place. Clara had probably never been there.

Virgil had let his last love slip from his hands; he was going to die alone. And too soon. He would have liked to get old before dying, have his hair turn white, his skin wrinkle, and his bones snap. Like sexual relations, death requires preliminaries. Fatigue, disillusion, and illness are the caresses and kisses that loosen our muscles and allow death to carry us away gently. Virgil wasn't ready; his capacity for producing suffering and tragedy hadn't been exploited enough.

The time for assessments had come. If he had to describe himself, if he had to describe the man that the world was going to lose, he would have said the following:

He was thirty-one and weighed 159 pounds. He always dressed the same way: dark corduroy pants, a V-necked sweater, checked shirt, English shoes. His cell phone was an old model, solid enough to endure the inevitable daily drops. Three times a week he took a yoga class in a gigantic gym on place de la République. Sunflowers were the only flower he bought or gave. The films he watched were all in black and white, and when a film in color interested him, he adjusted the television to get rid of the color. He listened solely to records, drank chic-

ory, and used a single kind of pen, an orange Bic with a
black point. When it came down to it, he liked things
that had lived: clothes, films, books. Old things had endured; inside them, they had an experience of life. New
objects hadn't attained puberty; they didn't understand
a thing about our loneliness.

Virgil worked for an advertising agency located on
the rue Saint-Honoré, not far from the Louvre. He lived
in a building on the rue de Dunkerque that was used to
turn tricks, just opposite the Gare du Nord and its statues. A porn theater, the Calypso, was on the ground floor.
Of the sixteen apartments in the building, fifteen were
for exchanging money and fluids. It had taken time to get
used to the constant moaning of prostitutes and their
customers; nowadays they didn't bother him any more
than the music of crickets in Provence. But few yells,
cries, and growls came from his own apartment. His
death would have serious consequences, he knew; the sci-
ence of disasters of the heart was going to undergo a serious slowdown.

Casting its rays on what was left of his meal, the
moon descended into the axis of the railroad station
clock. Records and books were spread across the parquet.
Virgil's pants lay in the kitchen. He had filled a dozen
glasses with wine (long and wide, with thin stems;
bloated, triangular, and shaped like a pear; chiseled,

plain, and frosted) and had stationed them everywhere, like sentries. From time to time, at different latitudes and longitudes of the building, the prostitutes' customers would cry out in pleasure.

Benny Goodman was performing "As Long as I Live." Virgil placed the answering machine on his knees and listened to the message once more. "Virgil. It's Clara. I'm sorry, but I'd rather stop here. I'm leaving you, Virgil. I'm leaving you."

He felt the full weight of the disappointment in Clara's voice. He hated himself for having been the cause of her sorrow. The state of his health didn't matter to him anymore; he was feeling guilty. In the little time that remained, he decided to behave honorably and acknowledge complete responsibility. He was unaware of the reasons for the end of their affair, but they weren't difficult to guess; he didn't like taking vacations, he was snide about everything, he didn't believe in anything, and his habit of contradiction was exasperating. He understood Clara's decision. He wasn't made for relationships. She must have tried to change him. He'd resisted.

His telephone rang ceaselessly. Thanks to Faustine, the news had traveled through the grapevine of his galaxy of friends. It had circulated from Barbès to Gambetta, by way of Stalingrad and Strasbourg Saint-Denis. His friends had learned about the separation and his fleeting love affair at the same time. No one had known about his relationship with Clara. Virgil decided not to worry his close friends and to keep quiet about his amnesia, his disease. He invented a believable story about meeting the young woman at Maude's party, and about their too-short relationship. He confessed, "Yes, we were in love, but I'm too complicated, she'll be better off without me."

He cried about himself, about his inability to love, about his lost love.

Since he was still able to do it, he made up his mind to settle his affairs, cancel his subscriptions and service contracts. Next, he needed to reveal his misfortune to someone anonymous, tell about his anguish. He dialed his phone company.

It was then that Virgil discovered ending a contract with a company was like ending an affair; the rep wanted to know why, asked for a second chance, tried to sway him by offering presents. When Virgil revealed his condition and the uselessness from now on of having a telephone line, the rep informed him that the telephone would be cut off at the end of the week. The sound of her fingers hitting her computer keys grew sharper. Virgil imagined her with bloodred nails and hair done up in a bun. She had a quota of customers to deal with. Her supervisor was keeping an eye on her. She wished him a good evening and hung up. Virgil had been faithful to that phone company for years; he was expecting a little sentimentality. He should have been smarter about arousing emotion, regret.

He dialed the electricity company. A woman answered. Her mature, gravelly voice suggested a certain age and a cigarette habit. Fatigue and emotion were making Virgil's voice tremble. He was sprawled at the foot of the couch, his forehead covered with perspiration. The living room was feebly lit by the kitchen light. The women questioned him about his reasons for terminating his agreement.

"I've been stricken by a serious illness."

The woman mumbled. Virgil realized that she wasn't apathetic. He forced himself to cough. Tears flowed down his cheeks. The woman's fingers had stopped traveling over the keyboard. She was listening. Virgil abandoned himself to the pathos of those moments. Drunkenness was allowing him to bear up to the tragedy. He felt himself going very far.

"I hope I've been a good client."

As best she could and in an uptight voice, she said she was there and ready and willing to keep listening. Virgil wasn't complaining. In a serious tone he told her that he'd accepted his date with destiny. That he'd gotten used to the idea.

When he hung up, he felt capable of announcing the news to his close friends and making them feel they'd miss him. He even possessed enough *amor fati* to console them. He opened the third bottle of wine.

After sorting through his papers and mail and putting them in order, he wrote the termination letter for the lease for his apartment in a dignified style. Virgil didn't think of himself as a hypochondriac, but for several years he'd been afflicted with symptoms that were so disturbing that several times he'd thought his last hour had come. He therefore had a small stock of wills already drawn up. He printed out the one with the most recent date (adding a handwritten note asking that his ashes be scattered in the women's dressing room at the Auteuil swimming pool), slipped it into an envelope, and placed it on the mantel.

Even if you're stricken with the worst disease, the doctors will never treat you with one-tenth of the respect with which they honor viruses, infections, and thromboses. A body forms the setting where biologists, radiologists, and surgeons enter into communication with the only fascinating things on this earth: bacteria and other deadly micromonsters, whose complexity ridicules the most advanced of our creations. Despite his continual progression within the school of destruction, despite his talent for wounding, demeaning, and poisoning, man is still an amateur. His crude methods lack art in comparison with the infinite inventiveness of diseases. Our civilization needs further improvements so that it can someday claim the title of endemic.

Virgil couldn't bear hospitals. He found it telling that the places in which people were supposed to be kept from dying lacked beauty and life to such an extreme degree. The suffering caused by our sense of aesthetics had a purpose: these delinquent architectures promoted a certain idea of humanity that he found tasteless. Whenever his bank account made it possible, Virgil deserted the treatment centers for the community of mortals. Certainly he believed in the defense of public services, the involvement of the state in the economy, raising taxes—but his conduct was closer to an aristocratic individualist's than an alter-globalist's.

He refused to be an obedient sick person by visiting his GP, going for an X-ray for all and sundry, holding out his social security and insurance cards. To counterbalance such cerebral damage, he needed delicacy, charm. When you have the means of spending a small fortune, not only do you get an appointment quickly, but the doctors think of you the same way they think of themselves— very affectionately, in other words.

The radiology center was in the Marais, a few steps from the Musée Carnavalet. Virgil couldn't have dreamed of better surroundings; inside this museum was the history of Paris, from the vestiges of the Lutetians to art nouveau. Medicine can't function fully unless the unguents of human creation are attached to it. The molecules of pharmacopeia aren't enough; the treatment must also show an awareness of the homeopathy of Houdon's marble bust of Voltaire, Fragonard's paintings, or a Bach suite for cello.

The façade of the radiology office was magnificent. Virgil saw a poem in each element of its construction: *abba* rhyme schemes, caesura, enjambments; he grasped the form and the cadence. Sometimes the art of architecture was crude. Today he was discovering a marvelous poetry in the dressed stone, the friezes, and the carved balconies. The master builders and the occupants had a taste for beautiful things. The façade was provoking superb emotions in Virgil. He felt a bit better.

To alleviate his collapse, he'd dissolved an anti-anxiety tablet under his tongue; the fear hadn't disappeared, but remained a quiet kind of fear. Virgil kept his hand around the box of tranquilizers at the bottom of his jacket pocket. He pushed open the door.

"Hello, sir."

The receptionist knew the spiel for appointments by heart; he'd spoken to Virgil as if to a regular at a hair salon. It was fun. Virgil relaxed the pressure on the box in his pocket. Pooh-poohing convention, he shook the receptionist's hand. The latter wouldn't forget his handshake, nor would he forget his deep, melancholy gaze.

The office didn't smell like the usual hospital; it was filled with the odor of coffee and roses. On the walls were black-and-white snapshots of animals of the African savannah. Opposite the receptionist's desk, a half-circle of chairs upholstered in raspberry-colored fabric took the place of a lounge; art and antique magazines lay on a low table. Behind the counter, a series of photos of potted flowers had been set on a shelf.

"I'm early," said Virgil. "It'll give us some advance on the spread of . . ."

He pointed to his skull. The secretary smiled and suggested he wait in the lounge. Virgil sat down and thumbed through a magazine about altarpieces and other objects of religious art.

The doctor, a big woman in a white blouse and fawn-colored leather boots, appeared a few minutes later. Her eyes were light, her lips painted with pink lipstick. Everything about her face suggested benevolence: her dimples, eyelashes, nose, the convexity of her big forehead. Every facet of her being contained the potential for kindliness. She spoke about the test as if talking about a simple routine. Her sweetness was impressive. In her presence, nothing could be dire; if she announced imminent death to somebody, the event would lose its tragic aspect.

"I don't want to be kept alive by artificial means," warned Virgil as he followed her down the corridor.

He was already imagining his body in the whiteness of a hospital bed, tubes going in and coming out of his mouth, nose, veins; surrounded by purring machines, a respirator, an electrocardiogram machine, his parents at his bedside, a vase filled with flowers.

"We're going to do a test, there's no risk."

A window separated the CAT scanner and the

computers used for analysis. The doctor detailed its functioning. Virgil didn't understand a thing, but the oral rundown of the machine helped calm him. He tried to convince her to give him a general anesthetic. She thought he was joking. He didn't insist.

He liked the CAT scan. Due to a sort of professional deformation, as soon as he saw an object, he couldn't keep from thinking how he'd present it to make it attractive. It was indispensable, every household needed one! A good ad campaign coupled with mass production could make all that a reality.

A nurse went with Virgil to help him climb onto the table, and injected him with contrast dye. During the scan, to calm him, the doctor told him the story of the invention of the CAT scan. The doctor was part of a species that was on the way out: the cultivated humanist. She was behind the window and speaking into a mike. A small loudspeaker was located above the CAT scanner. The voice of the doctor filled the cold room with the story of Godfrey Hounsfield, genial do-it-yourselfer, a scatterbrain obsessed with his research. At the beginning of the 1950s, he joined EMI, the record and electronics company. There he perfected the first computer to use British transistors. It was an achievement, but the innovative machine didn't interest anybody. Because of its commercial failure, it was put on the shelf, and he was transferred to the central research laboratory. That was the moment when the Beatles had their first worldwide success, which filled the coffers of EMI. Taken aback by such unexpected wealth, the directors left Hounsfield, their mad scientist, to himself. He was free to do the research of his choice, to devote time and money to it. That was how Hounsfield ended up working relentlessly on his ideas. One day, concluded the doctor, he achieved the hoped-for result: he linked an X-ray tube with a computerized data-processing system. In other words, he'd invented the CAT scan. Virgil enjoyed the story; it had the force and beauty of an ancient myth: music coming from the farthest reaches of death.

Intense heat flowed through his face and skull. His hair vibrated. He was flattered by this human and technical display on his behalf. He felt important. He thought of the years of research necessary to invent the machine, the engineers, the doctors, the slow death of Marie Curie as a result of the radium she was handling without protection in the shedlike laboratory of the École supérieure de physique et de chimie industrielles in Paris.

When the scan was finished, the nurse led Virgil into an adjacent room. The doctor had hung X-rays on the view box. They looked like abstract paintings. The light added a velvety softness to the gray shapes. Virgil examined their dark masses and the holes. An encephalitic termite had hollowed out tunnels in his brain. He was finished, he figured, as he held his head between his hands. His mouth was dry, the blood pounded in his temples, and his vision grew blurred.

"Everything's okay," said the doctor as she placed the film in a large envelope and handed it to Virgil.

When you fear the worst, the simplicity of the announcement of good news is disappointing. Virgil would have liked hoorays, confetti, hugging and kissing, a speech, champagne; he wanted the staff in the office to celebrate the event for what it was worth.

"Are you sure?"

"I don't joke about this kind of thing."

"Can I get a second opinion?"

"I'm a doctor," she said with a smile, "I'm not interpreting sacred texts."

Virgil was a tad disconcerted by the fact that his brain didn't require more skill; that his complexity wasn't going to induce debate among specialists at international conferences and articles in medical journals. However, despite appearances, and despite his own perceptions, he was okay. He was relieved and simultaneously shamed at not having had more nerve. Now that all the danger had passed, he squared his shoulders and pasted on the expression of a guy who's sure of himself. He thanked the doctor and paid the receptionist, then walked out with a nonchalant wave of his hand.

It took three buses to get to the passage des Petites-Écuries. During the trip, Virgil reacquainted himself with the idea of living; he appreciated the simple movement of his breathing, from his lips to the bronchioles of his lungs. Everything seemed different, endowed with a completely new feeling of three-dimensionality and luminescence: pieces of paper on the ground, the gray of pigeons, billboards, cars. He was seeing for the first time. The concept of the ordinary had disappeared from his personal lexicon; reality seemed directed and decorated by a surrealist artist. In thinking that he was losing his life, he had temporarily lost the world. Now he was rediscovering it, more present than before, realer and more beautiful. The CAT scan had served as an incubator for the premature baby that he'd been for thirty-one years. He'd gained strength, his immune system had been reinforced, his senses had gained nerve cells.

As soon as Dr. Zetkin had closed the door, Virgil told her the news: "I don't have anything."

The psychoanalyst didn't seem surprised. But from

her point of view, Virgil was suffering from something: this episode was going to revive the issue of hypochondria. According to Virgil (and Dr. Zetkin probably didn't share his theory), his hypochondria was more of a hobby than a neurosis; when you're a bachelor, with all that time wasted not having sex, not strolling through the woods hand in hand, not going to the movies to see a big-budget romantic film, there are no activities more stimulating than getting X-rays and electrocardiograms and undergoing various clinical gropings. Dr. Zetkin filled her cup with tea. The steam lightly fogged her glasses.

"I thought I was sick, that my memory was playing tricks on me," said Virgil without bothering to sit down.

He placed his hands on the desk and leaned toward the psychoanalyst.

"Actually, that girl had a good time leaving a message on my answering machine. Then she called Faustine to tell her that she was leaving me. It's Machiavellian."

"And why would she do such things?"

"She must be nuts."

"You see craziness everywhere. That's how you avoid confronting complexity."

The observation stunned Virgil. He tried to reply, but he couldn't think of anything pertinent to say. The psychoanalyst got up and opened the door, apparently

satisfied with the state of confusion in which she was
leaving her patient.

A fine rain was falling on boulevard de Strasbourg. Those
hawking roasted corn were sheltered by umbrella hats,
the hair salons were full, people were talking, having
coffee. Virgil took off his jacket. He was in a hurry to
find Armelle and get her advice.

He walked with a light step, staring into space. The
rain falling on his skin felt good. He hadn't escaped
death, but, for a while, the idea of death, which was direr
than death itself because it hounds us our entire lives.
Every medical test result made it possible for Virgil to
undergo a resurrection and take fresh delight in the
world. Even if his hopes for life kept projecting farther
and farther into the future, he lived in the same state of
anguish and fragility in relation to his body and to disease as a man of the Middle Ages; he had no doubt that a
simple cold could turn fatal.

Virgil's life was well organized. He distrusted meanderings of his thoughts and tended to force them to
calm down, the way you'd bring a wild animal to heel.
Concluding that this woman was crazy allowed him
to seal the issue. But Dr. Zetkin had instilled some doubt
in him.

If Virgil examined the situation objectively, he had to admit there could be reasons other than insanity. This frightened him and aroused his interest at the same time. As he walked up the boulevard de Magenta, he thought of Clara as a kind of complicated mathematical problem. The bus stopped. Virgil climbed aboard and took a seat at the back.

He started to list the possible explanations. He drew a column at the back of the book that he kept in his pocket. He chewed on the end of the pen and gathered his thoughts. It was highly improbable that this was a joke. They were past the age of telephone pranks. Also, it wasn't funny. A narcissistic wound followed by vengeance? At the party he paid no attention to that girl, and because it had angered her, she'd played this trick to get back at him. He was gentlemanly, but absentminded enough for such a faux pas. He thought of sending her flowers. When the bus stopped in front of the Gare du Nord, he still had no answer, but the problem didn't really interest him anymore; he was full of pleasure at the thought of his return among the healthy.

It was time for lunch. Rain dropped from the sky in translucent shards. Located opposite the stately entrance to the station, the Terminus Nord was never empty. Businessmen and Belgian, British, Dutch, and French tourists were eating their first meal in Paris or drinking their last cup of coffee at the counter before the departure. Suitcases were wheeled across the mosaic floor to wait next to tables like docile domestic animals. There were as many men and women in suits as those wearing casual clothing. Oysters were shelled, waiters rushed from table to table loaded with trays of seafood; the smells of the sea mingled with those of the café. The regulars were eating at the counter or in the small lounge at the back of the brasserie.

Armelle was outside, drinking a Perrier. Her way of waiting had lots of charm, distinction. Virgil would jiggle his leg, drum his fingers on his thigh, shift his feet and head. The young woman was tranquility itself; her body wasn't in her way, her mind functioned without bunching up her flesh. She waited as if she were carrying out a noble activity, an ancestral art that was complex and refined.

She was wearing a thin, black, hooded coat over a white cotton tunic; a plum-colored silk scarf around her neck ran under her lovely hair. Several books poked from her handbag.

The two friends had gotten to know each other in philosophy class at the university. Moved by a sudden inspiration, Armelle had sat down next to Virgil in the lecture hall during a conference on Stanley Cavell. They'd related immediately as they discussed the big mural by Puvis de Chavannes, an allegory representing the sciences and the arts in the form of some brightly colored characters and some muses. It was an antidote to the six statues of depressed, serious masculine figures that had been stuck into the niches of the lecture hall.

During that amazing journey that was their first conversation, Virgil had fallen in love with his fellow student. When she informed him that she was lesbian, he displayed the great timing to kneel on the ground and ask her to marry him. After several benders, they had become inseparable. Armelle was in her own category; she didn't belong to the same world as Virgil's other friends; she didn't know them and showed no desire to meet them. She had her own friends, whom Virgil didn't associate with, and Anne-Élisabeth, her girlfriend, who lived in Strasbourg.

Armelle wasn't academic enough to hope to get a

degree in education and teach someday. Shortly after finishing her doctoral dissertation (*The Will Not to Be Understood in the work of Nietzsche*), she began posing for erotic magazines (she was tired of student jobs). Seeing her first photos had upset Virgil. Her face was unrecognizable, because she was good at making herself up. Makeup, wigs, colored contacts, jewels, temporary tattoos allowed her to preserve her anonymity. Nudie magazines, lingerie catalogs, and Internet sites scrambled for her image. Being a faithful and conscientious friend, Virgil would go with her to Studio Daguerre for the photo sessions. Under his bed he kept a copy of the magazines in which she appeared.

Armelle put most of what she made in the bank and lived in a maid's room on the rue de Maubeuge near the Gare du Nord. Every day she went to class at the Université libre d'astrologie et des sciences occultes in the basilica at Arts et Métiers. Since her academic achievements would never gain her access to a decent profession, she had pragmatically decided to believe in the influence of heavenly bodies on human beings, and to become clairvoyant. One day Virgil had asked her if she actually believed in the occult. She'd answered, "Of course, since I've decided to."

There was no bragging in her assertion; her conviction was subdued yet unshakeable. Virgil knew nothing

at all about his friend's past, but he'd noticed the scar
from an old wound on her left forearm, and sometimes he
caught a fleeting gleam of despair in her eyes, a trace of
melancholy on her lips. These signs of sadness would disappear, and Armelle would regain her lightheartedness
and humor, but Virgil suspected that she was returning
from far away. She needed some sort of grounding. It was
vital. The fact that this grounding was a fantasy, a crude
myth, an invention made her more solid and more stable
than it would have if it had belonged to the real world; the
geology of her world depended only on that.

It was a waste, Virgil had thought for a long time,
somewhat like a soprano abandoning her opera career to
sing on television. Armelle had mastered Latin and ancient Greek; her historical and philosophical knowledge
was phenomenal. She was, of course, agnostic. When
Virgil pointed out the lack of scientific foundation for
clairvoyance, she replied that advertising proved the per-
sistence of magical thinking and the irrational in modern
society. No one escaped having beliefs. At least astrology's
pretensions were disarmed by its bad reputation. Once
Virgil had tried to bring her back to shore, to a reasonable
activity; he had assured her that divination had more to
learn from her than the opposite.

"So much the better," she answered. "As long as it

offers some advantage for those who come to consult with me."

By the light of a small lamp at the Bibliothèque nationale, during her studies at the University of Astrology and Occult Sciences, she'd learned the history and the techniques of *divination artificiosa* as she would have learned to play the piano, with the same determination and the same enthusiasm. Clairvoyance had become her instrument; using it, she assimilated music theory, scales, the different styles and forms of the discipline: dream divination, astrology, palmistry, fortune-telling, chresmology, crystal gazing, hydromancy, catoptromancy, pharmacomancy, arithmomancy, dowsing, geomancy, numerology, and graphology. She mastered intuitive divination at the same time that she absorbed the divination of the learned.

Virgil ended up agreeing that Armelle's project wasn't lacking in meaning or appeal. He understood that it was an expression of his friend's vital force. The type of clairvoyance envisioned by Armelle was no whim, but an honest passion. She worked tirelessly to understand human beings and to find a way to present her knowledge in the form of the language and practice of divination.

The big clock on the station read noon; the bells in the Église Saint-Vincent-de-Paul pealed. Virgil sat down next to Armelle. Grasping the back of his neck, she drew him toward her and kissed him on both cheeks. Her perfume (Tubéreuse Criminelle), hair, and gaze had an immediate effect on him. His shoulders fell, his neck relaxed.

"You okay?" asked Armelle.

"You know, love and death."

October was taking an interesting turn. Virgil had escaped getting sick, and a mystery was looming in his life. He ordered a *croque-monsieur* and a salad and recounted the events of the last twenty-four hours.

"Now," he concluded bitterly, "I'm going to look like an idiot."

"I think it's a beautiful story," said Armelle.

Virgil's love life was an important subject of conversation among his friends. The news of the end of his nonstory of love was going to supply them with entire evenings of material. So Virgil made a decision that surprised even him.

"I'm not going to say anything."

Armelle thought for a moment and acquiesced. "Nothing says you have to."

They looked at each other with conspiratorial delight, like two children who'd decided to play a fabulous trick. That was the answer. Christianity had established the concept of truth in our minds with profuse torture and the courts of the Inquisition. But as soon as we renounced burning witches, hunting down Jews, and justifying slavery, lying seemed much more appropriate for life in society.

"And since everybody thinks your heart is broken, they're going to make a fuss over you."

"True."

Virgil's group of friends saw him as a victim of feminine cowardice, a gentle lamb sacrificed on the altar of the implacable relations between the sexes. For twenty-four hours, his friends had been calling, asking how he was holding up, offering to go to the movies with him, and inviting him out to dinner.

"You're going to see if you can find out why this Clara tried to make you think that you'd been together?"

The waiter brought their plates, the salad bowl, and a carafe of water. The smell of the gruyère in the gratin distracted Virgil for a moment. This was his first meal since the CAT scan; the *croque-monsieur* would be the best he'd ever eaten. His senses were intensified, his sensitivity at maximum capacity. He covered the *croque-monsieur* with lettuce leaves sprinkled with minced shallots and parsley.

"I already have enough trouble understanding the normal things people do. It's just a girl saying she broke up with me, who left a message on my answering machine in order to . . . I don't know and I don't care. It's all the same to me."

"You're not very curious."

Virgil's hand swooped down on the alarm clock at 7:31 AM. He was in spectacular form. He went through his drill: yoga exercises, then shower, then breakfast (bowls of oats with soy milk, yogurt, dried figs, and bananas). He left his apartment at eight-thirty and ran into the neighbor, who lived on his floor, as she was bringing up a customer. The velvety light of day caressed him. He said hello to the three girls on the sidewalk, and hopped onto the bus.

The bus was full, and he ended up between two ladies who were discussing the international financial crisis. At every turn or even gentle sudden stop, he fell on one or the other. He arrived as the offices at Svengali were opening. Nothing was forcing him to be punctual; he had no time clock, no one exercising strict control over his schedule. Virgil followed the rules as soon as none were being imposed; free will was the condition of his obedience. His hours (nine to five) provided a framework for his days; work for him was boxed inside a temporal prison.

Because of the countless legal problems of his parents' circus, he had acquired sensitivity to justice early in life. For that reason, as soon as he landed his baccalaureate, he'd registered for law school. But an academic orientation turned him into a zombie. Virgil was bored to death. To keep from plunging into a permanent coma, he began to audit philosophy classes. This choice didn't do the trick. Very quickly he faced the facts: his grades on the civil and administrative law exams destined him for a low-ranking, low-paying job, an insecure and unrewarding position as an office worker, or, at best, a notary's clerk. He didn't come from a family of Brahmins, and the lumpen proletariat was welcoming him with open arms. His imagination was his life preserver.

Advertising was the only sector where a young man with a gift for ideas could find refuge, lead a lone life with days that were relatively free. He'd sent his résumé to several agencies. Svengali Communications had given him an interview during which he was ill at ease enough to convince the director of human resources that he had an interesting personality. That same person was also impressed by his double major as well as his talent for forging his diplomas, and he was recruited for a job as a copywriter. Of course, socially this put Virgil on the grill: only the makers of antipersonnel land mines have a worse image. The young man became the laughingstock of his friends. He had to put up with the jibes of those who were better born and worked in sectors that had a veneer of respectability.

In a spirit of pessimistic contradiction, he eventually developed a cynical argument in favor of advertising. The longevity of brands, he'd point out, surpasses that of marriage. They offer a feeling of continuity, confidence; they're the menhirs and pyramids of modernity. And if people don't believe in brands, what can they believe in? In ideologies that create millions of victims? In love, which is going to take the piss and vinegar out of them? In a godless world, where love affairs don't even last two years, consumption helps you cope without your getting involved with the collective.

Svengali had been founded a century and a half ago by the grandparent of the current coexecutive (her husband sat next to her on the board) at a time when industry was booming. The building had been built three years before the French Revolution, across the street from the Comédie-Française, which had opened a short time before. The woodwork was redone after the Paris Commune, but the dominating mentality was more connected to Thiers than to Louise Michel. Svengali had approximately fifty employees distributed throughout its three stories. Posters and photos for the agency's campaigns by Toulouse-Lautrec, Mucha, Vuillard, Fellini, Cassandre, and Piatti were hanging on the walls.

Svengali was Virgil's cocoon. He loved walking its corridors, working in the staffroom to the sound of the coffee machine, listening to his coworkers, sometimes adding a word or phrase to a conversation. He had no office, just a cubicle in what was dubbed the Idea Room. The notion of limiting ideas to a specific place amused him. A small plaque that said IDEA ROOM (like the kind used for the lavatory or for a conference room) had been attached to the door with screws. It was a pleasant place. You wrote on a large blackboard, read, sketched, and discussed.

Virgil got along well with his coworkers, even if he was making an attempt to see them as protoplasmic animalcules. For convenience's sake, he practiced Levinas's philosophy: the face of the other prohibits murder and is a remembrance of the existence of the human community. He didn't expect anything from anyone; consequently, they enjoyed a peaceful coexistence.

Virgil had a certain respect for Svengali. It wasn't one of those agencies full of too highly paid young people with cocaine-stuffed noses and a disdain for consumers. Certainly they weren't saving any lives; they went to great pains (with a blatant taste for come-ons) to con the public into buying things it could do without.

The premises were comfortable. The management worked at preserving an outdated tradition of elegance. No bright colors, no electrically operated doors, no fluorescent lights. The offices were in mahogany and the chairs in leather; the old parquet floor was impeccable; the interior design would have excited an antique dealer. Coming to work in sneakers, or driving a car that was too powerful and showy, would have been looked upon very unfavorably.

Lately Virgil had been brainstorming a campaign for yogurt—ordinary yogurt, but produced by the number-one food processing industry in Europe—which was to say, he had to find things about it that were incomparable. His mind was teeming with lactic images of cows, meadows, dessert spoons.

An odor of patchouli incense floated out of Simone's office. The door was open. Masks, farming tools, dolls, wall hangings, and rugs decorated the room. Several times a year, Simone went to a third-world country and came back with lots of tchotchkes to furnish her cave of Ali Baba. She encouraged the copywriters and graphic designers to use them for ideas, shapes, colors. The world had volunteered to become their paint box and alphabet; it was enough to spend several minutes in this bazaar of an office to benefit from the influence of its treasures.

Simone's visitors sat in leather armchairs in front of a bay window. It offered a view of the pont des Arts leading to the buildings of the Institut de France and its Académies. Simone was the manager of a department, but she had no need to act like one. Her natural authority, sense of humor, and the simplicity of her behavior sufficed.

When Virgil appeared at her door, she invited him in by a downward flourish of the albino peacock feather in her hand. The young man sat in an armchair. To excuse his absence of the day before, he invented a plausible story about a case of hives that had something to do with a skin ulcer (a *noli me tangere* or don't-touch-me kind, he specified, cloaking his lie in something serious and poetic). Simone wore an orange-and-yellow Indian-patterned skirt; her hair was held back with a coral barrette. Virgil had been in love with her since he came to Svengali. Two things had put an end to his enthusiasm: she was his boss, and she wasn't interested.

"We thought of you for the position of senior copywriter," she told him.

Virgil wasn't expecting this. For those used to disastrous report cards and papers peppered with corrections and reprimands from teachers, there's something unreal about a promotion. Since his first day at Svengali, he'd been happy to throw out ideas; he'd never led a campaign. He had the soul of a scout, not a general. He took the feather and shook it in front of him, thinking about the death of the peacock and about its feathers scattered throughout the world. Simone liked the fact that he was surprised; she lit another stick of incense.

"It comes with a raise, of course."

The tip of the incense stick glowed red. Virgil didn't think for very long before responding.

"That's nice, but it doesn't mean anything to me."

"You're joking," replied Simone.

She let out a small yelp when the match burned the end of her fingers. Virgil was embarrassed, because he valued Simone. By turning down her offer, he felt as if he was acting rude, or rather, tactless. He blushed, then re-affirmed his position.

His refusing to let his salary go up a few figures amazed Simone. In an advertising agency, a creative person had the benefit of a certain tactical margin: he had the right to be lost in his thoughts, to wear odd shoes, to listen to Korean rock while banging out the rhythm against a bowl with a wooden spoon, and to consume all the substances he desired. But Virgil's behavior out-stripped the limits of acceptable eccentricity. Simone asked him if he still was not feeling well. He reassured her that he was. Suddenly he no longer looked like the polite, gifted employee she'd thought he was; he was an exotic creature she'd discuss during the next manage-ment meeting, a specimen she hadn't had to bring back from Africa.

Virgil went back to the Idea Room. The place had a large stained-glass window. Virgil sat down at the center table, grabbed a piece of paper, and armed himself with an orange Bic with a black point. He jotted down a series of words, put his chin on his folded hands. As soon as his mind focused on work, he felt okay. His life was just too pitched; he desperately needed a return to stability. He worked to get the sensation that he had when he expended effort, and only for that. He had no desire to climb the ladder of success. Not that he found it absurd or reprehensible; it just wasn't his cup of tea.

He'd spent his existence trying not to be noticed. It was a matter of survival. Being noticed brought two dangers: you laid yourself open to getting whacked, and to being overlooked. It was wiser to stay in a twilight world without any glory.

Virgil often thought about Marcus Aurelius. When he'd won the battle against the barbarians of the Danube who were threatening Rome, he wasn't overwhelmed by happiness, but by despair. Victory wasn't a solace. Virgil was sure of it: in life you have to do your best at not losing and not winning, at the same time. Putting this into practice is tricky, since both poles have strong powers of attraction.

Her red silk skirt lifted gently by the wind, Faustine waited in front of Pho Dong Hu'o'ng, a Vietnamese restaurant in Belleville. If your thing is watching a marriage played out in overkill with the sizzle of flashbulbs, listening to love songs in Mandarin, and sampling refined, exotic dishes piled onto carts pushed by waiters in white, go eat on the second floor of the President. But if you prefer a quieter setting, the humble Pho Dong Hu'o'ng is for you.

Faustine leapt toward Virgil and pulled him tightly against her bosom, a gesture he never grew tired of. They sat down in the back of the restaurant. This was their canteen. The waiters threw out a little small talk to them, the food was good, the service competent, the prices modest, and the customers mostly Asian. The menus were written in Vietnamese, but there were pictures of the dishes. Whatever you chose, you weren't disappointed.

Virgil had met Faustine during a performance of *Twelfth Night* at the Théâtre National de la Colline. Actors dressed like robots spoke in computerized voices and moved around in tiny flying saucers that they wore around

their waist. Virgil had had an attack of the vagus nerve
five minutes after the curtain rose. Luckily, Faustine had
been sitting in the same row and caught hold of him
before his head hit the floor; she led him out of the theater. A sugar cube and a glass of water helped him get
back on his feet and fall in love with his rescuer (who was
dressed for the occasion in an outfit of black organdy and
a lovely pair of checkered pumps). But Faustine didn't
remain single long enough to give him a chance to declare
his passion. Winning her heart required the skills of a
sprinter, because suitors were falling over one another to
get to her. Virgil had little interest in or aptitude for com-
peting; he renounced any romantic claims and they
became friends.

"Holding up?" asked Faustine.

"It isn't easy."

Virgil gazed down with a beaten expression. Inside
he was glowing. He was about to do what he spent his
days doing: concocting recipes of words and emotions.
What's more, he had experience playing the guy who'd
been dumped; he knew all the complaints and every
detail of the routine.

Faustine had known about the "separation" before
everybody. If she was a friend of Clara, she would have
known that the relationship had never existed. But that
wasn't the case. Virgil made up his mind not to look any

more deeply into it, so as not to arouse any suspicions in his friend.

The waiter appeared at their table, his pencil poised over his pad. Virgil claimed that he wasn't hungry. Faustine insisted. He ordered three beers. His friend canceled the alcoholic order and put together a gourmet meal. Virgil let out a sigh when the waiter brought a *banh khoai* (turnovers with pork, shrimp, and bean sprouts), with a crust that was puffed and golden. He pretended that he was forcing himself to eat the delicious *cha ca* (fried fish), the *bun thang* (soup), the *nems,* and the *chao tom* (sugar cane stalks with shrimp). He was delighted by the spicy flavor of the cumin, *nuoc-mam,* and grilled peanuts. He carefully hid his pleasure under various painful frowns.

Faustine thought that he had a lot of guts; he wasn't moaning or launching into any bitter rants. For the first time in his life, her friend was suffering with dignity and wasn't indulging himself. She couldn't get over it.

During the entire meal, she tried her best to change his thinking. That's why she was nice enough to tell him about her last fight with her partner. Nothing consoles a single person better than stories about couples. Individually, Faustine and her boyfriend were attractive. Together, they were a convincing advertisement for vasectomies and tube tyings. The combination they made had few vestiges of the beings they'd been before their fusion (in the strange world of love relationships, fusion led to fission).

The message Faustine was sending Virgil was clear: couples suck. If there's an end to history, then it wasn't caused by the advent of Napoleon, as Hegel had thought, or by the fall of the Berlin wall, as conservative intellectuals thought, but by the reign of the couple: you're right on track, and the next event in your life will be your death and you won't get any announcement. Faustine expended a lot of energy convincing him of the futility of love.

Dinner finished with a cold, sugary drink of many colors, made from a gelatinous plant stock, with bean sprouts and coconut milk. Faustine took care of the check. The evening had been super.


International laws, a kind of Verona Convention, protect broken hearts. These laws are supported by a powerful brotherhood. Every evening Virgil was taken care of. People took turns babysitting; they went out with him, fed him, massaged him. He was invited to the theater and the movies, to openings and cocktail parties. It was impossible to accept every invitation. Very quickly, matchmaker types started talking to him about attractive women.

Life had never been so wonderful; he was benefiting from the effects of breaking up without any of the inconveniences. During his earlier romantic failures, his unhappiness had prevented him from taking advantage of the comfort that came along with them. To really enjoy the recovery process, realized Virgil, it's better not to be sick.

From conversations, he was able to deduce that none of his friends had spoken to Clara. Some of them thought they'd met her at Maud's party, but no one remembered her. She had definitely been there, but there was nothing else they would have been able to say about her. She wasn't part of Virgil's circle. So there was no risk of his being unmasked.

Nadia invited him to spend the weekend in Normandy at the country house of her fiancé's parents. Usually Virgil hated these visits far from civilization, with people he didn't know and whom there was a good chance he wouldn't like. Group experiences totally turned him off. Predictable conversations about things you were obliged to talk about drained him. He had nothing original to say about politics, sex, or the weather, and he detested revealing his intimate thoughts in front of people whose only purpose was to reveal theirs. But since he didn't want to hurt Nadia by keeping her from consoling him, he went along.

Friday evening he climbed into Nadia's fiancé's green minivan, which was decorated with stickers (flowers, animals, rock groups). The seats were foam rubber; there was no headrest and the inside was filled with a persistent odor of stale vomit. Obviously the vehicle had never passed an inspection, and the driver belonged to a belief system that let him ignore the need to keep a safe distance; consequently, Virgil was surprised by their getting to Houlgate alive two and a half hours later. Nadia introduced him to the people he'd be spending the weekend with. There would be eight of them in the large house. Before dinner Virgil went for a walk on the beach.

The visit didn't go as he'd feared. They asked nothing of him. He didn't clear the table or wash the dishes. He spent a lot of time on the couch in front of the fireplace, immersed in a novel. He was the only one who chose the music (there was an old record player and an exciting, dust-covered collection of King Oliver and Bix Beiderbecke). He enjoyed some great Burgundies, ate the best cheeses (camembert with calvados, livarot, and some pont-l'évêque). He made no effort to participate in conversations, and no one dared contradict him when he came out with peremptory judgments about a film or book, or when he claimed to be a Keynesian in favor of euthanizing trust-fund kids and abolishing inheritance. He'd answer a question by sighing or shrugging his shoulders without offending anyone. It was normal procedure to give him the largest piece of pie (made from apple and black currants from the garden, its crust rich in butter and sugar).

Virgil's misanthropy had faded away. He was discovering that the human species had one use: to serve him and be at his disposal.

*S*unday evening, when he got back to Paris, Virgil (satiated, tired, stuffed, a few pounds heavier, with a thin layer of salt on his skin) wandered through his neighborhood. The lights of the food stands on rue de Dunkerque, the last surviving porn theater, cafés, and brasseries did him good. The evening was coming to a close, couples were going home or arguing, taxis were filling up, street cleaners swept the sidewalks.

He met Armelle again at the Terminus Nord. She was wearing a pair of dark blue jeans, a tailored white décolleté blouse, a thin, open-necked sweater in beige merino, and a black wool jacket. Women and their clothing fascinated Virgil. They made him think of chameleons eternally searching for the color that would allow them to blend in with the world. This perpetual quest for a new look made them impossible to grasp. A man doesn't have many clothes; he has no need for camouflage and becomes attached to what he has. A man comes to light in his clothing, but the world comes to light in a woman's. Virgil ordered a glass of Almaviva, Armelle a glass of Gevrey-Chambertin.

"It's absurd," said Virgil, "but I've never been so happy."

Armelle pulled a card from her tarot deck and placed it facedown on the table. It was a beautiful deck, decorated with hieroglyphics. She turned the card over: a monk carrying a pair of scales.

Tradition, Armelle had explained, considered the tarot to be a historical mutation of *The Egyptian Book of the Dead;* it went back to time immemorial. Virgil replied that resistance to time was no proof of the validity of an idea; stupidity has bloomed quite impressively over the course of centuries. Armelle parried the attack by quoting Plato (*Phaedrus*) and Cicero (*On Divination*), both of whom believed in soothsaying. According to them, certain people had access to hidden truths and decoded the world like artists. That was the case for Armelle. Sensitive and visionary, she had incredible gifts of observation and deduction. As if in a waking dream, she deciphered souls.

Every time that Virgil found himself in a difficult situation, he was tempted to call upon her talents as a clairvoyant. But that would have meant admitting that he granted some credibility to the hoax. He was afraid of putting his friend in an awkward position if her predic-

tions didn't come true—and putting himself in one if
they did. Anyway, Armelle had told him that it was impossible to practice clairvoyance with someone close to
you, because your feelings confused the interpretation.

Virgil may not have believed in the tarot, but that
didn't stop him from calling upon Armelle's sensitive
powers of perception. He asked her opinion about the
current situation.

"Ideally, happiness mustn't depend upon outside cir-
cumstances." The waiter brought the wine and a little
dish of salted peanuts.

"I get by the best I can," said Virgil, biting into one of
them.

"I'm sure you can do better than getting by."

She put a bunch of keys on the table. Virgil took a
moment to examine the little mailbox key, the safety-
lock key, and a big gold key. Finally he understood.
Armelle had bought the office where she intended to
practice her nutty activities. It was a plan that went
back years. Something positive was happening in his
friend's life, and this filled him with joy. They left the
café arm in arm.

The office was located on the fourth floor of a building of classic beauty with a view of the canal Saint-
Martin. Virgil hadn't realized Armelle was making such
a good living. For six years she'd been saving her earn-

ings (most of which were paid under the table) from posing nude for photographers. It wasn't surprising that it had ended up as quite a haul.

Armelle hadn't only bought an office; an adjoining apartment was part of the take. It had a living room, kitchen, bathroom, toilet, and two bedrooms. The entrance opened onto a vestibule with a sofa and several small chairs (the waiting room, explained Armelle). A dormer window let some daylight in. On the walls hung photographs, prints, and drawings having to do with the occult sciences. One door led to the office, the other to the apartment. The living-room floor was bleached wood. The room contained a large trunk (on which had been set books and candlesticks), a sideboard, and a coat rack with spidery arms. Cast-iron bookshelves covered the walls; some of her books had already been arranged there, but most of the shelves were still bare. The kitchen's most appealing feature was its large tiles, which depicted the signs of the zodiac. The two bedrooms were equipped with rattan furniture. The cupboards and drawers only held a few things. Armelle had transferred the contents of her 100-square-foot spartan maid's room to an apartment ten times larger.

The office was splendidly decorated; the walls were upholstered with carmine red wall hangings, and a Venetian mirror stood opposite a window. A portrait of

Orpheus had been hung near the bookshelves. Armelle would minister to her clients at a damask-covered table. On it she'd placed osselets, a golden ring threaded with a piece of silk twine, and a crystal bowl that resembled an enormous eye. An open cabinet near the window revealed various bric-a-brac used in the practice of divination. On a hanger attached to a plinth hung Armelle's costume, a black and mauve dress and a shawl embroidered with little pieces of broken mirror. Books on spells, arcane texts, and handbooks on palmistry were arranged in the library; esoteric pictures had been placed right on the floor.

Virgil went down to buy a bottle of champagne at the grocer on rue des Récollets, perpendicular to the canal. It turned out to be undrinkable, so they clinked empty glasses. Virgil was proud of his friend; with patience and planning, she'd invented a life. After hugging Armelle and inhaling the jasmine perfume in her hair, he left so that she could take care of the final details of moving in.

He walked north along the canal Saint-Martin. The sun was setting, and close to the Jaurès subway station, the canal was tinged with red. His face in the water blurred under the intermittent drops of rain.

As soon as Virgil opened the door to his apartment, he noticed the absence of the little red light on the answering machine. He pushed the light switch; the electricity had been cut off. A week had passed since he'd canceled his contract. He didn't feel up to explaining his sudden recovery to the power company. He found some candles under the sink. The flames would give the apartment a Gothic feel.

The ceiling was trembling. The neighbor above was entertaining a customer. Despite the great number of matches he sacrificed, Virgil couldn't light the waterlogged candles.

When the box springs on the fifth floor stopped creaking, he went upstairs. His neighbor opened the door, dressed in a white bathrobe with a red rose embroidered at breast level, her forehead covered with perspiration, a can of Coke in her hand. She didn't have any candles. She insisted on lending him an old cave explorer's helmet with a lamp on the front.

Once he was on his couch, Virgil put the helmet on his head, attached the strap under his chin, and lit the lamp.

The light illuminated the bookshelves. As soon as he moved his head, the beam shifted. He turned on his cell phone. A feeling of immense weariness beat down upon him.

For his friends he was playing Unhappy Man without being unhappy, and that turned his grief about the loves of the past into something grotesque. By mimicking his customary behavior, he'd realized what a caricature he was: someone who was constantly dissatisfied, who parroted the same complaints without ever taking a good look at himself. He was grateful to Clara for having allowed such an insight. He was fed up with the failure role he was so talented at playing. He was less equipped for happiness, but he was determined to persevere in this asymptotic direction.

Without his expecting it, Virgil's malaise had gradually given way to the sweetness of solace. He wasn't made for lying. What's more, he didn't like the way his friends talked about Clara. They didn't know her. Out of loyalty to him, they were being unfair to her. Virgil had had a fantastic week, but the farce no longer amused him.

He took a can of sauerkraut from the cupboard above the sink. He hadn't done any shopping for ages. It was the first evening in a long time that he was alone and eating at home. He set out some silverware on the low table in front of the couch, stuck his fork into the can of sauerkraut, and sat down opposite the television. The lamp on his helmet lit up his lousy meal and its reflection bounced off the gray screen. He ate to the sound of orgies erupting around him. The fermented cabbage and poor-quality meat liquefied into cold acidity in his mouth, but he didn't care.

Virgil got up and wandered around looking for God knows what. The light attached to his forehead revealed fragments of his apartment as if he were exploring a cavern with cave paintings. Spending the night at a friend's and hearing any unbearable words of consolation was out of the question. He decided to take a walk.

As if he wanted a little company, Virgil unplugged the answering machine and carried it against his chest. He walked down the street and settled at a Terminus Nord table. Tired customers with drawn features were waiting for their train. After ordering a cup of herbal tea, he plugged the answering machine into the electric outlet under the banquette. He pressed the SAVED MESSAGES button.

For some obscure reason, Clara's voice moved him. He needed to hear it.

The answering machine remained silent. Virgil pressed the button again. He put pressure on the black plastic with his finger. Nothing happened. It was hopeless, he realized; some nameless engineer had decided that saved messages would only be archived for one week. Even technology was part of the plot. Clara's disappearance stepped up a notch. The only proof of her existence had vanished. Virgil wished he had the nerve to put the answering machine on the ground and kick the plastic to smithereens. The screws would pop out, the thin tape would unwind like the entrails of a dead animal.

The herbal tea had cooled down. He missed Clara. He missed that woman he couldn't remember. For twenty-four hours he'd thought they'd had something; he'd imagined their love with sincerity. Then he'd spent a week pretending to weep over their separation. With amazement, he realized that the revelation of their non-relationship didn't erase the construct of his attachment. As if playing at being brokenhearted actually had fractured his heart.

We spend our life clinging to people who are easy to get, to loud people who make themselves noticeable, while others remain off to the side, there in the shadows. But we make no effort to go to them. Virgil had met a woman, and he couldn't remember her. Nobody could remember her. It filled him with despair.

Clara was like a ghost: Virgil had no proof of her existence, and, in some way, she haunted him. The older he got, the more ghosts were becoming his reality, because they gave meaning to the world. Trying to understand the universe and human relations without them seemed like a pipe dream to him.

He called some friends to find out if any of them had taken photos or shot film at Maud's party. No, for once no one had bothered. He paced back and forth in his small apartment roaming agitatedly from room to room. Simply to have something to do, he put his English ankle boots on their shoe forms and polished them.

The doctor at the radiology office had given him the X-rays from the CAT scan. Virgil took them from the envelope marked with that unsettling symbol for radioactivity.

His brain was displayed in eight sections as if it had been hacked into slices by a butcher. He taped the X-rays to the window. The apartment grew darker as the brightness of the streetlamps and the moon diminished. The beam from the front of Virgil's helmet swept across the X-rays. Clara was in there somewhere. In those nervures, shadows, and jellylike masses, the memory of a young woman was hiding. Specks of gold floated in the ocean of neurons and synapses. Virgil brought his face closer. With his fingertips he caressed the contours of the gray matter.

Whether Virgil understood it or not, he felt drawn to Clara. His intuition whispered to him that he'd had some understanding with her during their brief encounter at Maud's party.

The confusion he was feeling expressed itself physically. His body was plaguing him. His muscles were contracted, the movements of his joints painful. He felt he was in the same state he would have been in if he'd been sailing alone for ten days on a raging sea. He went to his yoga class. The gym at the place de la République felt anonymous and cold. At that late hour there weren't many people. Virgil liked its factory ambiance. He wanted an impersonal place where he could get some rest from himself and stroll around in blue shorts and a black short-sleeved shirt, without the risk of getting involved in a discussion with some friendly person.

n the majority of cases, humans have immune defenses too effective to let them become open to love. There are those who want to slide into the bliss of a love relationship, but such people are small and weak, and will succumb to the attack of the antibodies. Unlike a virus, true love only comes into being for the benefit of inanimate things; the deader they are, the more the plans of our heart have a chance to find fulfillment. Monuments, works of art, old cities are our only way of knowing the joy of emotions that last.

Virgil's friends were all part of a couple; some were married, others had bred. The time for experiments was behind them. They were waiting, out of friendship and conformity, for Virgil to find a relationship that would last indefinitely. But he wasn't so sure he wanted to be like them.

Falling in love has some very grave consequences. Together you plan for the future, move in together; eventually there are children. Then, given Parisian real estate, there's a great risk that the couple will vanish into the suburbs.

In loving a woman, Virgil was taking the risk of losing

his great love: Paris. His attachment was easy to explain. When you've experienced the cultural, human, and aesthetic wasteland of small towns in the suburbs and provinces, Paris becomes an oasis. You don't need to have grown up in Paris to be in love with the city, just as you don't have to have been born poor to appreciate the value of money. Virgil had spent his life thirsty; he had a vital need to live near a fountain.

Of course, Paris was expensive, stressful, less and less working class; the traffic was difficult and the air was polluted. But it still had more movie theaters and pharmacies than any other city in the world. Besides, Virgil loved the endless appearance of students, people out of work, wage earners, retired people, illegal immigrants. As he saw it, there was no better way of getting to know the capital than by mingling with that fun-loving, combative crowd. Those colorful, ragtag parades made him proud of his city. He saw them as beautiful floral outbursts on the asphalt that got in the way of cars, brought the normal life of whole neighborhoods to a temporary standstill, and pulled the police from their vans. A city of complainers and protestors, a hive of upheaval, Paris was never as real and beautiful as when it was resisting.

Seven years earlier, when he'd signed his job contract at Svengali, he'd gotten out of the lease on his maid's room on boulevard de Strasbourg. His parents had come from Bourges, where the circus would be for some time, to help him look for a place to begin his life as an independent adult. Virgil lied to them about his salary (which was so ridiculously high he was ashamed); consequently, they'd gone to look at small apartments in posh neighborhoods that were unfit for habitation, miniscule apartments fit for habitation in lethal neighborhoods, and a lot of apartments requiring them to wait in line and produce exorbitant references. After a lot of disappointments, they'd unearthed the apartment on the rue de Dunkerque. Quite probably, the real estate agent was having a hard time getting rid of it because he didn't raise an eyebrow when Virgil's parents revealed their profession and started demonstrating a few of their tricks. Tired of apartment hunting, Virgil signed the lease. For one thing, living near a major railway station was reassuring for a claustrophobic type like him.

He liked the diversity of the neighborhood. In that northern part of the tenth arrondissement, foreigners (Indians, Arabs, Chinese, Africans) lived and worked in great numbers. The tectonics of the continents were at work thanks to these foreign languages, clothes, colors, smells, and foods. Virgil discovered that the world was more on the move here than it was elsewhere; continental plates collided, had encounters, overlapped, the landscape was in perpetual mutation; hills, ravines, mountains, oceans loomed inside consciousnesses. Among its peculiarities, the neighborhood had a concentration of two paradoxical elements: an unbelievable number of bridal shops and almost as many porno-flick booths. Romance and pornography: a perfect summary of human aspirations. Virgil loved the geographical and fantastical ellipses of his surroundings.

However, since he'd moved here, he'd seen a transformation at work. The real estate developers and authorities were methodically destroying the urban fabric with their repainting, renovating, rebuilding. Rents were climbing; the poor were moving to the outskirts or living in smaller and smaller apartments. Neighborhood associations were clamoring for a greater police presence and launching petitions against the prostitutes and bums.

Virgil didn't speak to most people in the neighborhood or to the merchants on his street; he had no interest in community life and street fairs. The other 2 million inhabitants of Paris disregarded him, but the city was all his; he merely had to put up with them. The owners, developers, lawyers, real estate agents, court officials were powerless to do a thing about it; Virgil couldn't be expropriated or evicted. He walked around as master of his domain, the keys to the city in his pocket. He was at home on benches along the avenues, in parks, on bridges, and in old buildings, on square Léon and the tip of île

Saint-Louis. He'd place his hand on the edge of the Saint-Michel fountain with the feeling that it belonged to him.

His friends lived in the tenth, eighteenth, nineteenth, and twentieth arrondissements. That was the Paris of their daily life, their cafés, their movie theaters, and their restaurants. In those places there was still the illusion that money hadn't conquered everything, even if they themselves were contributing to the increase in cost per square foot by renting and buying their small apartments. They belonged to a hard-up class of intellectuals who were still being helped out by their parents; when they weren't getting unemployment, they worked in theaters, museums, on documentary projects, and in art publishing. Nothing in the world could have convinced them to make appointments in the bourgeois neighborhoods of Paris.

When Virgil arrived at the Gare Montparnasse at the age of eighteen, he'd decided that Paris was going to be his love object, because you really do have to focus your love on something. Paris wouldn't leave him. Paris was there when he needed it. Paris wouldn't make him go away on vacation to some island paradise, to beaches where the suntan lotion made you sick to your stomach. Paris wouldn't care if he didn't do the dishes for a week, didn't shave, or dressed badly. Paris loved him.

*T*hings got back to normal. Monday looked as if it were going to be as futile and uneventful as usual. A week had passed since Clara's message.

Virgil would begin his day with a green tea, then follow it with cups of chicory. The drink had a nice color, and he was used to its flavor. The electric burners still weren't working. Virgil opened the fridge. He held his breath to keep from inhaling the foul odor of rotten eggs and fermented tomatoes. The yogurts had turned into cheese; bacteria had caused the plastic containers to swell like hot-air balloons. He couldn't keep surviving in the shadows on cold beverages. He called the power company and asked them to turn the electricity back on. The service rep explained to him that it wouldn't be easy: because of his death, his file had been closed, sealed, and sent to the archives department in Guadeloupe. Virgil would have to come up with a medical certificate and wait for the exhumation of his account by an ad hoc committee. It would take two weeks. Until then, he'd have no other choice but to take showers at his health club or at Armelle's.

At least he wasn't cold, he noted as he put on his pants. Heat wouldn't be necessary for some time yet. Thanks to the tons of carbon monoxide coughed into the atmosphere by monster automobiles, autumn was late in cooling down.

Virgil's bad mood and confusion were leading to some morbid thoughts. He remembered certain winters from his childhood when the heat wasn't working and there was no hot water. He'd sworn not to live like that anymore.

To blot out the flood of pessimistic thoughts, he took refuge in some yoga exercises. He bent his legs, did a shoulder stand, slowed down his breathing. After a half hour, the tension subsided.

He went down to McDonald's for breakfast. He didn't think he needed any more than an acidic orange juice and a greasy piece of pastry. He left out the tea bag and drank the hot water. The other person at his table, a little man with a moth-eaten golfer's cap, a two-week growth of beard, and a dirty shirt, was eating fries and drinking a soda. His hand rested on a chocolate cake as if he were protecting it. Virgil wouldn't have admitted it to anyone, but he liked coming to McDonald's. It wasn't a pleasant or attractive place, but he felt at home there. If Hemingway had landed in Paris today, he'd no longer have the means to go to the cafés he went to in the 1920s.

The only haven where he could sit down to have a coffee and work would be McDonald's. Nowhere else could you take refuge somewhere warm for hours at a time, for a modest sum. The poor, students, people from the projects on the outskirts of Paris, are well aware of it; they check their e-mails, study for exams and classes, write; the homeless read the daily papers for free while pretending to drink from cups they've lifted from a tray. The concept of a refueling place for people of modest means had been abandoned for a caricature of capitalist enterprise. Fast-food places were now the only welcoming, lively environments that were open to the people. It was depressing.

When Virgil got to Svengali's offices, the receptionist told him that Simone wanted to talk to him. Virgil had just bought several pounds of different kinds of yogurt (with fruit, fruit-flavored, with active cultures, whole milk, fat free, with soy, sugar cane, chocolate). Inspiration demanded to be fed. The few ideas he'd already come up with hadn't won any support. He'd written a small paragraph that he would have liked to see on subway billboards, or, better yet, recited by a smiling actor in a TV commercial: "Yogurt is a symbol of the pathetic nature of human existence: it's colorless, tasteless, and full of bacteria, but it's one of the rare things we want that we can actually have."

After knocking on the half-open door, Virgil walked into Simone's office.

"They're insisting," she said.

The "they" she was talking about were the managers of the agency; Virgil sometimes saw them in the elevator. They were an attractive couple in their sixties. He'd noticed that the woman wore nothing but bright-colored tweed suits, with pockets shaped like open fans, and a single gold button for closing the jacket.

Virgil placed the yogurts on the desk. Simone was wearing a boubou, a straw hat decorated with a red ribbon and a stuffed hummingbird, and black satin pumps embroidered with metallic pearls. She was arranging exotic fruits on a copper plate. Virgil liked her a lot. He liked her face and its expressions of seriousness, certainty, confidence. Simone would blow her top about nuclear proliferation and deforestation and stand up for unregulated capitalism with a human face. She reminded him of a woman absolutely outraged by malaria who nevertheless belonged to a militant organization for the defense of mosquitoes. At the agency, political disputes were like friendly farces in which adversaries clashed without really being against one another. This seemly spectacle contributed to Virgil's peace of mind. His fellow workers would have been as comfortable under Stalin as under Reagan; like all patricians, they would have adapted to any regime whatsoever. This impressed Virgil, because his parents and their friends were the exact opposite. He loved them for that, for their inflexibility, but he was sorry for the isolation and suffering associated with it.

His hand grazed the exotic fruits. He caressed the lychees, persimmon, mango, guava, pomegranate. After hesitating, he picked up a passion fruit and tossed it from hand to hand.

"If you give me that promotion, I quit."

He was surprised by his own determination. It embarrassed him to rebel against sweet Simone; but he was feeling an unusual, overwhelming delight in self-assertion, in discovering that he didn't have to acquiesce to plans that had been made for him. He was shaking like some juvenile delinquent during his first robbery.

"Virgil, be reasonable," said Simone, with all the sweetness in the world.

"I don't see why I should. Nothing in my contract says I have to."

He wanted calm, routine. The least change risked collapsing the fragile structure of his existence. He thought about going to the unions to defend himself. Why should he change? He wasn't going to be corrupted by their ideas of ambition. He was working because it was a way to survive, not to succeed. He would have liked to explain to Simone that he'd found work in an ad agency partly because of his habit of using language to avoid becoming a target for people he had to face. During his years in school, he told stories and made his pals laugh so they'd spare him. But Simone wouldn't have understood.

"You're doing an excellent job," she said as she placed her hand on his arm.

"I'm not doing it on purpose," said Virgil as he left the office. "Think of it as collateral damage."

He was being sincere. When he was in Svengali's offices, he was in a children's park. He played with words and ideas and came up with slogans; he told tales whose characters were deodorants and cars.

Sometimes he happened to walk over to the Musée de la Publicité, which was close to the agency on rue de Rivoli. The windows, which were as large as doors and painted black, kept you from guessing at the piles of objects and posters that were in the display cabinets. Two floors documented the archeology of consumerist propaganda. It was a good way of reminding yourself that the shelf life of advertisements was no longer than that of flowers. Virgil liked that fragility. The superficiality of these products kept you from taking yourself seriously. It was a lot of noise (money, people, and meetings) signifying nothing. There was something moving about creating these fireworks.

As the years went by, Virgil had begun to regard advertising in a detached way, as an object of study. His understanding of it and his observations had led him to associate it with the category of "ephemeral architecture." Three examples of that artistic nomenclature seemed to him to correspond to his professional activity.

1. Joseph Paxton's Crystal Palace: an immense, prefabricated structure in glass and steel around sixteen hundred feet long, built at Hyde Park in 1851.

2. During the Renaissance, painted wooden panels that were stuck to the façades of houses (the ones that were ugly or too common) during religious or princely marriage processions.

3. Catafalques and other temporary mortuaries: works of art, found in most cultures, which disappear in the flames when the dead are incinerated.

Advertising combined these three actualities: an arrogant display of riches and know-how, a trompe-l'oeil, and a funeral pyre for destruction. Virgil liked such polysemy. In something apparently very trivial, he'd found food for thought and for dreams. It helped make his situation bearable. For years his work had been a good way to acquire knowledge. Under the pretext of looking for ideas to recycle or the inspiration to sell soap, razors, and diapers, he'd use his expense account for novels, art books, films, CDs, concerts, and plays.

When Virgil got to the Idea Room, he unpacked yogurts and piled them on the table until he'd reproduced King Djoser's Step Pyramid. The original had been built five thousand years ago by Imhotep. Virgil walked around it and studied it from different angles. The steps were supposed to allow the king to escape to heaven. Virgil placed a yogurt at the top.

That day at the agency was horrible. Time seemed to crawl. As if he had been infected by Clara's disappearance, Virgil felt the bonds between his molecules disintegrating. Under the subdued light of the stained-glass window, in the shadow of the yogurt pyramid, on the blackboard with chalk, he drew cows with furious eyes, their gigantic horns pointing toward the sky, their udders hanging past their flanks. To the sound of a Kenny Arkana album, he leafed through some magazines, wrote haikus, and threw balled-up pieces of paper into the wastebasket, the way an American basketball champion—he fantasized—would do it. Usually, just pretending to work was enough to get to work. But nothing good came from his orange Bic with the black point. He ate different kinds of yogurt, hoping it would inspire him. All he got out of it was a strong feeling of nausea.

Advertising isn't art, but sometimes, when the sponsors had big ideas, it was possible to create some pretty little things that weren't overly stupid. But since Clara's message, or since the threat of his promotion (he didn't know which event had changed his frame of mind), Virgil had lost all desire for these trivial creations.

His colleagues weren't wasting any time. Discussions, the opening of cans of soda, and various exclamations created music that was very much like a song of labor. If his coworkers had consulted one of the dictionaries located under the boxes of Ladurée macaroons, nougats, and brownies, they would have found out that etymologically, *consumption* is destruction; or to put it more precisely, it is leading something to destruction by exploiting its substance. Virgil wondered if his choosing this profession was a way of accomplishing a nihilistic act, like a timid Nechayev, author of *The Revolutionary Catechism*, because through it he was participating in total annihilation in a way that was more effective than bombing. The ideas he came up with had consequences. Consumption was increasing; factories were functioning at full capacity, which meant waste was being produced in the form of cardboard packaging, plastics, toxic substances. Earth was being joyfully poisoned, the glaciers were melting, atolls were disappearing, catastrophes were multiplying, the rarity and price of oil, like the wasting of raw materials, were undermining political balances. Through his work, Virgil was applying one of the precepts of Nechayev: encourage chaos to undermine society. Destruction is necessary for the advent of a new world.

He was suffocating. Impossible to open the window.
In vain he looked for the box of tranquilizers in the
pockets of his jacket. He felt like he was in danger, surrounded on every side. His mind was being attacked by
a kaleidoscope of images of graves, cemeteries, bombs
dropped from planes, troops of Falangists, gunshots,
camps, barbed wire, Guernica, families in tears, ghosts.
He left the Idea Room, threaded his way along the wall
of the corridor, took the service elevator. He passed under
the DO NOT ENTER sign stretching across the stairway
leading to the roof. The caretaker was on vacation and
had given Virgil a copy of the keys so that he could water
his beds of thyme, mint, and chives.

When the metal door opened, the sky suddenly appeared and the weight on Virgil's chest lightened. The
air up here was easier to breathe; there was less noise,
too; and no one, no one was looking at him.

Virgil paced, got his wind back, recovered his calm.
He squatted and touched the damp soil of the large rect-
angular pots. He cut off a leaf of mint and tore it. A bead
of scented sap formed on his thumb. He brought the leaf
to his mouth and chewed it. Images of mint tea, Armelle,
a deck of tarot cards, his parents went through his mind.

He leaned on his elbows against the edge of the roof
and looked out over Paris. As if escaping from an old
vampire film, a mist covered the city. At the horizon,

black clouds were approaching. He'd never found clouds like that menacing. He liked darkness, rain, and the occasional flash of lightning that they brought.

Gusts of wind beat down on the roof; dead leaves, pieces of paper, small amounts of rubbish scuttled about. Virgil's hair ruffled. He shifted a pot of thyme and found the caretaker's box of cigars, wrapped in a damp, torn, filthy bath towel. He lit a small cigar, a Partagas panatela that had already been smoked three-quarters of the way down.

The roof had been converted into a heliport, but the restrictions on flying over the capital had kept it from being used. A fine layer of moss covered the white paint of the landing strip; red fire extinguishers had been placed all around; there were a first-aid kit, a pilots' and mechanics' handbook, and some tools for helping passengers to get out in case of an accident. Virgil liked the idea of a helicopter landing here. He imagined climbing inside. The most difficult thing wouldn't be the takeoff, but finding a place inside that was safe.

He was getting a little high from the nicotine. He sat on the ground and leaned back against the ledge. The glowing red of the cigar between his fingers recalled the crater of a volcano boiling with lava and ready to explode. He took a puff; the thick, white smoke escaped from his mouth and was dispelled by the air.

Thoughts cartwheeled through his mind. They made him aware of something very unpleasant: aside from Armelle, his friends bored him. So many times during a dinner, at a party, while leaving a movie, he had wanted to say, "We already had that conversation, don't you remember?"

Inevitably, there comes a moment in a group when each person finds his place. Virgil was the sarcastic, eccentric guy. His friends were used to his chronic depression and to the annual spectacle of his tragicomic loves. He'd played this role to be accepted and loved, to have people around him and be understood, to participate in the reassuring perpetuation of the same things. And his friends played their own roles in the drama without questioning their script or character. Why didn't they drop out of sight for a while, for God's sake? Didn't they see that becoming a ghost was the best way to exist? Virgil wanted to stay on the roof and be taken in by one of those clouds arriving at the horizon. Maybe, by disappearing, he'd find Clara again.

At that moment, he resented her. It astonished him to realize it, as he would have suddenly become aware of an enormous splinter stuck in his hand that he hadn't noticed until that moment. Rage bubbled up in him. It was an emotion that was foreign to him. But there it was, even if it did feel awkward, even if he didn't know how to express it: he was damn mad. Why had she behaved that way? What right had she had to meddle with his existence? What had come over her?

The cigar was almost finished. The live ember warmed Virgil's fingers. His mouth was full of residue: strong, acrid flavors, as if he'd eaten warm earth suitable for cultivation. He put the thick brown butt in a place where it would go out by itself. A bit of smoke was still escaping from the outer leaf of the cigar.

Using a headache as a pretext, Virgil left the agency. He drank a large decaf at Á Jean Nicot. The restaurant-café reminded him of the establishments he'd gone to with his parents when he was young. Virgil's mind was empty. The manager said something to him. He didn't understand and shook his head. His mind and his tongue seemed paralyzed. As if only his legs would work, he left and began to walk.

He didn't like this neighborhood, its useless stores, the quantity of noisy cars, the people passing by. This was the Paris he hated. This was the Paris that wasn't Paris any more, but a gigantic shopping mall. The Libraire Delamain was a refuge. He went inside, walked up and down its aisles. The ceiling was high, the atmosphere hushed, the lighting soft. It had a lot of old books. With his hand he caressed the rows of novels. His index finger stopped on an edition of Théophile Gautier's *Roman de la momie*. Virgil's situation was like that of the arch-aeologist who fell in love with Queen Tahoser, whom he had discovered in her tomb: an impossible love for a missing woman. He'd been intending to buy the novel, but put the book back when his eyes met those of a clerk. An old terror grabbed him. He was afraid that the man at the register would refuse his money because he wasn't worthy of the store, not worthy of having the money and using it as he pleased. As if he were always the child in a shop in an unknown city, holding tight to the precious coins in his pocket.

He left the bookstore and climbed on the bus that was going to the Gare du Nord.

When Virgil got off the bus, he didn't walk in the direction of his apartment. He went into the station. The immense concourse and the glass roof had a strong effect on him. A voice announced the departure of a train for Brussels. A man was running on a platform. Virgil was tempted to follow him, to dash up beside him and climb on when the all-aboard signal rang out. To flee the city and start his life again somewhere else.

His feelings for Paris were no longer so strong. He was admitting something that had been unimaginable a few days earlier: the hazard of birth had placed him near a large, mythical city; but other cities were possible, cities like Berlin, Lisbon, São Paulo, or one of the eastern European capitals. He was thinking about the countryside, too, a place where birdsong and the sounds of bicycle wheels wouldn't be drowned out by the racket of cars. Paris seemed like a trivial luxury accessory, whose name sounded good and was easy to pronounce.

The doors of the train closed. The wagons were set in motion. As the train got farther away, picking up speed, Virgil understood that he'd ceased to dream. The autumn sun shone through the glass façade of the station. The coffee machines in the fast-food places were running nonstop; a fine powder of arabica coffee floated in the air. Virgil bought a decaf and sat down on a bench facing a track.

Since you can neither become happy nor give up wanting to be happy, he'd long ago decided not to be noticed, not to move, to avoid suffering. That period was over. He was going to change something in his life. He didn't know what it was yet, but he was going to act.

A half-hour later, as he sat on his bench watching the trains depart, his cell phone rang. Armelle was getting ready to see her last client; she was inviting him to come to her office. Virgil left the station.

The red lights of the restaurants and the white lamps of the streetlights got on his nerves. He would have liked all of them to go dark. He lowered his eyes and stared at his shoes as he walked. The regular movements of his feet along their path made him think. Each step represented one piece of a gigantic puzzle that he only became aware of after it was completed. When Armelle opened the door, he'd made his decision.

"I'm going to find her," he said.

His eyes were still lowered, a sign of the intensity of his thoughts. Armelle raised his chin and kissed him on the cheek. She closed the door and led her friend into the office.

"I miss her," said Virgil raising his hands in a gesture of helplessness.

"You miss a girl that you don't know?"

"There's nothing I can do about it."

"You look ready for a fight. It's nice to see you like that."

Armelle was taking him seriously. It was one of her wonderful qualities.

"I've spent my life avoiding trouble, and the result's a catastrophe. Why not take some risks for once?"

They went into the office. From a cabinet built into the library, she removed a bottle of Pic Saint-Loup and two long-stemmed glasses. Virgil took a swallow. The warmth of the wine did him good. Armelle told him about her clients. Word of mouth was working. For years Virgil had watched her focusing on the realization of her project; it was a kick to see her being so enthusiastic. They were the same age, but she was ahead of him. Nothing seemed to stop her. Her example gave him incentive. They went back to the subject of Clara.

"You don't remember if she was blonde or brunette?"

Virgil lay down on the couch. He needed to rest. Deciding to begin searching for Clara had drained him and unleashed a strong wave of anxiety, but he had definitely decided not to let himself be intimidated by these fears that commanded him to barricade himself at home.

"I don't know whether she's tall or short, I don't know the color of her eyes, don't know her political opinions. I don't know if she'll go to see old movies with me, if she reads, what music she listens to. But I love the way she talks, I love the tone of her voice."

Nothing seemed more important to him than that. Birdsong, music, the noise of leaves swept across the ground were an unpleasant din compared to Clara's voice.

"Why do you think I can't remember her?"

"The most common cause of amnesia is trauma to the cranium," said Armelle in her very distinctive tone of gentleness mixed with irony.

"I haven't been hit on the head."

"Well, you've had a shock, in some way or other."

Virgil palpated his skull. Armelle opened the window to air out the office. Secrets, tears, passions had accumulated in this room during the day.

"Everybody feels sorry for me," said Virgil. "I can't stand it. My friends spend their time pitying me. I can't take being looked at like a desperate case anymore. As if my coffin were waiting in the next room. It's not too late, I can still live."

"You're the bravest person I know, Virgil. I'm not worried about you."

Virgil got up and leaned out the window. Homeless people in front of their tents at the edge of the canal were singing, couples were pushing strollers, teenagers were playing Ping-Pong, a barge was waiting at a lock. A group of young people was picnicking.

"I like those tiny lights," said Virgil, pointing to dots forming what looked like a string of lights in the thickets near the lock.

"Those are young people smoking crack. They're hiding. Ever since the corner became the 'in' place, the cops patrol it a lot."

Virgil's eyes clouded over with sadness. Armelle pressed herself against him and put an arm around his shoulders. Virgil liked her tuberose perfume mixed with hyacinth and nutmeg.

"I'm going to give you some advice about Clara," said Armelle.

"Why not."

"Don't imagine her. Don't fantasize about her. It would be a fatal error. Because the day you meet her, you'll be disappointed."

"'Don't imagine her,'" repeated Virgil, trying to put the idea into his head.

"You don't realize it, Virgil, but you've got to defend yourself against the incredible powers of your imagination."

Armelle was right. Virgil dreamed up the women he loved. Not to mention, as well, that he loved them *because* he was imagining them. When he met them, he covered them with his portrayals, with features that didn't belong to them. If Armelle was so close to him, it was because she had enough substance and mystery not to set in motion this creative mechanism. There was no hollow to fill in.

Armelle's warning was unnecessary, however, because for once Virgil was confronting a woman who really was unimaginable. Imagination isn't born ex nihilo; it needs matter to transform. And Virgil had no clue available, not the slightest particle or pigment that he could have used to create a portrait of Clara. Certainly he could have drawn a perfect portrait; it would have been everything he wanted to find in a woman. But he was too informed about the risks of such an approach to go through with it. When we dream of our ideal partner, we spontaneously depict ourselves without lacks and weaknesses, and with the kind of genitals that are needed.

The day had vanished without Virgil being aware of it; he'd hardly done any work, and spent his time sharpening pencils and moving his belongings from place to place. This Tuesday evening, he was alone at Dr. Zetkin's. He sat in the same place, between the entrance and the door leading to the office. He took advantage of being alone to stretch his legs and slump in his chair.

The sessions with Dr. Zetkin had given him the chance to understand the extent to which his childhood had affected his love life. He'd passed his youth traveling across France with the Elephas circus troupe, which his parents were members of.

The circus had been founded at the end of the Spanish civil war by Emilio Lavinia, a member of POUM. In March 1939, Madrid was falling because of Colonel Casado's betrayal; the Republican army had been destroyed, and the foreign volunteers were going home. Franco's supporters were hunting down their opponents, among whom Lavinia and his comrades had taken refuge in a Catalan village near El Vendrell. Most of the buildings were in

ruins; the inhabitants had fled or were dead. On the village square, a circus had partially withstood the hail of
bullets and bombs. Emilio Lavinia and his friends sal-
vaged the big top, trailers, and costumes. They embroidered the name Elephas in place of the circus's original
name. There'd be no elephant or other exotic animals in
the circus; these fugitives were instead attracted to the
name and the figure of the pachyderm sewn on the
canvas. For them, the enormous animal was a symbol of
irony.

The circus allowed them to travel through the country incognito, and to take refuge in France. To keep from
arousing suspicion, they put on a show wherever they
stopped.

These men and women who'd left behind their pro-
fessions at the beginning of the civil war in order to learn
the handling of arms and explosives soon developed
undreamed-of talents as acrobats, tightrope walkers,
strongmen, musicians, contortionists, clowns, magicians,
and jugglers. And against all expectations, they turned
out to be just as good at performing as they had at fight-
ing. They got hooked on their new costumes.

Virgil's parents learned about Lavinia and his circus
when they came to Pau at the beginning of the 1960s.
Both of them had lost their parents during the German
occupation, and nothing was holding them back. They

dropped out of high school at Lycée Louis-Barthou to join the troupe.

The circus was a close-knit community. It included children, adults, the elderly, horses, a sheep, a donkey painted like a zebra, dogs, and cats. Under the effects of the accordion, guitar, and wine, the oldest told stories and recalled friends who'd fallen, battles, and the solidarity of their early years. But it was a difficult, insecure life. Some of the members of the troupe committed suicide; exuberant dinners concealed a general tendency toward alcoholism.

Revenue for the circus varied dramatically. In some cities, no one passed through the red and gold panels of the tent. The receipts depended on the weather, a soccer game on TV, or an epidemic of gastroenteritis. When the audience came in large numbers, the troupe lived reasonably well. When the audience rarely came, pasta took over the daily menu; good food from town halls and clothing from Catholic charities were always welcome.

They never lived more than a month in the same place. Virgil would stay at a school just long enough for the brawniest kid to spot him and punch him out.

His parents were a happy couple, but their routine had influenced his view of romantic relationships. At the sound of a drum and cymbal, his father, wearing a blindfold, threw knives at this mother (wearing a pink outfit with gold piping that was outrageously sexy) while she was attached to a giant spinning target. The blades would plant themselves less than half an inch from the maternal flesh. Virgil spent his childhood witnessing this potentially homicidal spectacle. He was divided between the terror of seeing her die and shame about her displaying herself in front of audiences often composed of friends from school and their parents.

According to Virgil, the two of his parents produced as much energy as a small nuclear plant. They were fatiguing, anxiety provoking, and he adored them. Since he'd moved to Paris, they'd sent him weekly postcards, usually a picture of whatever village square the circus was performing in. Virgil phoned them every Sunday, as well as whenever he had a nightmare in which his father missed his target ("Shrinks should give part of their earnings to their patients' parents," he'd told Dr. Zetkin). He made a much better living than his parents, but they wouldn't have accepted his money; so he'd created a fake organization (the Fortuna Houdini Cagnota, located in the fiscal paradise of the Cayman Islands) that sent them a check from time to time in a large gilded envelope because their birth date, name, or license plate number had been drawn from a lot.

This bohemian childhood explained Virgil's need for stability, why he didn't want to travel anymore and couldn't stand having financial problems, and why he'd appointed Marcus Aurelius, the Stoic emperor, his patron saint. The man had had to endure the death of his wife (as well as her possible infidelities), the betrayal of Avidius Cassius, and had defended Rome against the barbarians; his reign had experienced the flooding of the Tiber, the earthquakes in Cyzicus and Smyrna, and an epidemic of the plague. Day by day he'd struggled, but he'd survived, saved the empire, and lived as a philosopher. The empire that Virgil had to save was his own life. Two aides-de-camp were helping him valiantly and steadfastly in this enterprise: Dr. Zetkin and yoga. He always carried a copy of *The Thoughts of the Emperor Marcus Aurelius Antoninus* as a talisman.


The door opened, pulling Virgil away from his thoughts. He went into the office.

Dedicated as she was to her excellent practice, Dr. Zetkin showed no sign of surprise or interest when Virgil announced his project to find Clara.

"You're not saying anything," said Virgil, perplexedly.

Seated at her desk, her hands crossed over her notebook, Dr. Zetkin continued to look like a wax statue. The halogen lamp, dimmed to a low level, emphasized the shadows of her face. Virgil hadn't taken his usual place on the couch. He needed a face-to-face, not more talk about his dreams and free-associating ideas and images. He'd decided to put his psychoanalysis on hold. Dr. Zetkin seemed indifferent to this mutiny. Virgil would have liked her to speak, to say anything at all, it didn't matter what; but he needed proof from her that words had really come out of his mouth. He wanted to be sure that he'd been heard; understanding was secondary to that. From the promontory of her desk and the shelves of her library, Egyptian amulets and sculpted African heads seemed to be staring at him. This population from different countries and times offered him the reassuring feeling of being part of human history; his problems, doubts, and desires were part and parcel of a tradition.

Above the couch hung a reproduction of Raphael's *Saint George and the Dragon*. Good obsessive that he was, Virgil had spent a morning at the Bibliothèque nationale finding out about that figure. According to what he'd learned, Saint George had refused to renounce his faith and, as a result, had endured long, sophisticated tortures for seven years; he'd died and was revived three times before being decapitated. Virgil felt close to this character. The best-known episode in the knight's eventful life was the one in which he fought a dragon that was keeping the daughter of the king of Libya prisoner. In the

top right-hand corner of the picture, you can see the princess fleeing while the knight confronts the monster. The
painting gave Virgil courage every time he tackled a
problem. One question had caused him anxiety for a
time: why was the king of Libya's daughter running
away? Now he understood that she was leaving Saint
George alone with his dragon because she knew that
three was a crowd; the knight and the monster were prisoners of their violent relationship. Virgil preferred the
version painted by Paolo Uccello and exhibited at the
National Gallery, because there the princess was waiting
for the knight's victory. The death of the dragon meant
that she would have a place in his life. It was a romantic
vision that pleased Virgil. Dr. Zetkin finally decided to
break the silence.

"Do you feel that I ought to say something to you?
That you're wrong? That you're right?"

"Not at all."

Of course, the answer was really yes. Virgil wanted
her to take him by the hand and help him find Clara; he
wanted Dr. Zetkin to call her for him and explain to her
what a marvelous man he was. He felt pathetic.

"I'm going to take two weeks off."

Virgil was shaken by the news. How was he supposed
to get by without his three appointments a week? He
wanted to convince her to hang around, explain to her

that she wouldn't be disappointed by the show, that a story like this, sure to bring surprises and new developments, was worth the trouble of canceling her vacation.

"Where are you going?"

"You want to follow me?"

"No. Unless you ask me to."

Humor was a defense mechanism, he knew, but he was having trouble keeping himself from using it. He would have liked to make Dr. Zetkin laugh, but that was the same kind of neurotic ambition as wanting to make a blow-up doll have an orgasm. Someday he'd be mature enough to give up the idea of impressing his psychoanalyst. Someday he'd stop falling in love with women whose only function was leaving him.

"But you will have your cell phone with you?"

"No."

"Then what am I going to do if there's a problem?"

The worry was real. Virgil's environment was crumbling, and he was unsure of discovering anything else but emptiness once everything had unraveled.

"That's the question: what are you going to do?"

Dr. Zetkin was handing Virgil over to his own fate. He hoped she knew what she was doing. The next two weeks were blocked off in red in her appointment book. Virgil had one last request.

"I need a medical certificate saying that I'm alive so

that they can turn the electricity back on at my place. It's a long story."

Without any sign, without commentary, Dr. Zetkin drafted the certificate.

Virgil didn't have a very clear idea of his quest. Maybe he'd gotten carried away and was running after the idea of Clara, after the woman who represented the fulfillment of a masochistic fantasy: being left before even having a relationship. Maybe it was something else that he had to discover, a mystery he had to solve.

He folded the medical certificate and put it into the inside pocket of his jacket. It was a document that proved he was alive; Dr. Zetkin's signature and stamp attested to it. That wasn't bad news.

Faustine lived near the boulevards below Montmartre. She worked as a graphic designer at an art publishing house. Most of her leisure time and vacations consisted of participating in demonstrations to defend the rights of illegal immigrants and the unemployed, or setting up squats in middle-class buildings for those living in substandard accommodations. Among Virgil's friends, she was the one who had the most trouble doing her job.

As a way of remembering the reassuring atmosphere of Dr. Zetkin's office, Virgil had dumped loose tea into the pockets of his pants and jacket. He'd come directly from work; Wednesday had been dreary at Svengali. He knocked on the door.

Faustine opened it. She was wearing a khaki-colored dress and a black sweater; red and gold earrings dangled above her shoulders. She was magnificent. For Virgil, all women were beautiful. Those who weren't were simply badly dressed, with the wrong hairstyles and makeup. Men were mistakes of nature; there was no rational explanation for their brutish existence and lackluster physicality.

While Faustine put water to boil in a kettle shaped like an elephant, Virgil took off his ankle boots. They exchanged news and sat on the floor, at a cute little Japanese table.

Faustine bought, sold and exchanged a lot of things on the Internet. The furniture and ornaments didn't last any longer than her lovers. Virgil had a hard time knowing where he was in this apartment that changed appearance every month. The place where the couch was located held flowerpots a few weeks later; the bath became the kitchen; the bedroom turned into a living room; the library ended up in the cupboard for pots and pans. The WC was the only stable element in the large apartment; Virgil would hide out there when he felt an anxiety attack coming as a result of these mind-boggling transformations.

He was glad he'd never had a fling with Faustine. It wouldn't have worked. She was too unpredictable and too anchored in reality, too serious. These qualities had won him over, but very often what captivated Virgil in a woman turned out to be the very thing that doomed the relationship.

The elephant's metalloid trunk let out a whistle. Faustine got up and poured simmering water into a red porcelain teapot with black polka dots.

"You haven't been calling me much lately," she said.

Virgil had a feeling that Faustine was happy about his being single, because it made him available. For entire evenings she could talk to him about her lovers, her parents, her work, her projects. No one will admit it, but there's nothing to celebrate about our friends succeeding in life and falling in love, because it distances them from us. The most bonded groups of friends are based on romantic and professional failures. In this case, however, Faustine was wrong: Virgil hadn't called or seen her any less. She only had that impression in hindsight.

She served the tea in cups of glazed clay. It was obvious that what Virgil feared had happened. Faustine was surprised that he hadn't introduced Clara to her. She didn't understand why he'd been so secretive. She was vexed. In a month, he hadn't found the opportunity to organize a dinner, a drink.

Virgil could feel Faustine getting ready to unmask him. Male friends are easier than females. Women understand too many things. When it comes to their own selves, they're as myopic as a mole, but they see right through the games those close to them play. They analyze, interpret, comment, suggest. Men make do with simplistic, inopportune advice.

Since he'd begun psychoanalysis, Virgil had developed the habit of talking to his friends and keeping them informed about his romantic interests. This silence around the subject of Clara wasn't usual; Faustine was right. To dispel her doubts, he told her that he'd wanted to be sure of her feelings first. He treaded cautiously. Faustine seemed convinced by the argument. Now that all danger of the truth being revealed had been avoided, he told her about his decision.

"I've decided to win her back."

Virgil figured that his friend would be delighted with his romantic decision. After all, he was putting up a fight for once. In the past, every time he'd been dumped, she'd encouraged him to transform the breakup into a second chance, without success. That was because Virgil had been relieved about getting rid of women after he no longer understood why he'd been attracted to them. So he'd never followed her advice.

He brought the tea to his lips; Faustine threw a pillow at his face. The tea spilled onto his chest and scalded him. He cried out, taken aback, stared at Faustine.

"For years you've tried to teach me to put up a fight. . . ."

"I've changed my mind."

"You changed your mind?"

"You choose girls who inevitably reject you, just so you can confirm your paranoid isolation."

Virgil waited for the fatal blow as he wiped the tea off his face and shirt.

"Dump yourself by yourself, don't delegate it to others."

Not counting suicide or psychosis, there was, unfortunately, no way to dump yourself by yourself. With his fingers Virgil kneaded the tea leaves in his pocket. His relationships came back into his mind like figures in a painting by Hieronymus Bosch. Faustine wasn't wrong: he was his own worst enemy. He remembered his discovery of the triptych *The Garden of Earthly Delights* in a room at the Prado. Last year, Simone had made him take a vacation; she'd bought him a plane ticket for Madrid and reserved a room in a big hotel. Virgil hated leaving Paris; every time he traveled, the earth shrunk. It was inevitable. The feeling of living on a planet that it was possible to cover in a few hours horrified him. He needed to believe that America was inaccessible (and really was located near India), that China was packed with treasures and medicines, that Africa had civilizations adept at magic and forests full of mythical animals.

But partly to please Simone and partly because the incessant sexual comings and goings of his building were beginning to reach a fever pitch, he'd let himself be convinced. He passed the greater part of the time in his hotel, in the gilded wooden armchairs in the lounge, reading, playing chess with the one-eyed bartender, drinking tea in the gardens, and floating on his back in the pool among the international naiads. He'd convinced someone staying at the hotel who was a big fan of touristy visits and sightseeing to sell him the photos of his stay so he could show them to his friends and workmates when he got back to Paris. An ideal vacation, in short.

One morning he found a ticket for the Prado with his stuff, put there by Simone. The only thing he liked about museums was wandering around in them; he thought of them as kinds of forests where it was nice to take walks, daydreaming distractedly. Stopping in front of each of the masterpieces was out of the question. Virgil didn't have the ability to see more than five paintings in a row; beyond that was overdose; all those colors, subjects got confused. Klimt, Leonardo da Vinci, Marie-Guillemine Benoist, and Artemisia Gentileschi melted into one other in a kind of bouillabaisse.

To avoid the crowds, he'd gone to the Prado as soon as it opened. He'd covered the rooms, whistling; sometimes he stopped in front of a painting when his instinct told him to. He spent a long time studying Bosch's triptych because he recognized himself in certain figures that were being tortured, and several of his friends bore uncanny resemblances to the portraits of the damned.

Faustine served more tea. To relax things, she'd put on a jazz CD.

"Okay, you're right," said Virgil. "I've never chosen

women who could have worked out. But what happened with Clara changed me. She was different than the others."

"Really?"

"You wouldn't believe to what extent. I'm trying to understand why she left me."

Faustine pouted to express doubt at the idea of her friend's capacity to change. But she was moved by his determination. She revealed the four reasons, according to her, that could pressure a woman into splitting.

"You're a misanthrope, you don't believe in yourself, you work in advertising, and you live in a building for hookers. It's normal that women wouldn't be at ease."

They'd known each other for five years, but Faustine had always refused to come over to his place because of the degrading spectacle of the prostitutes and their customers. Faustine's principles were quite charming. It hadn't been for no reason that Virgil had been attracted to her.

"How was I at the party?"

"Like always: ill at ease and a sense of humor that was as sharp as a bayonet. You were drinking."

Virgil drank at his friends' get-togethers. Alcohol didn't make him any chummier, but gave a better quality and more confidence to his shyness and distaste for being sociable. His drinking didn't get that out of hand; he flirted with drunkenness without getting sloshed; it was a way of letting himself go completely while still maintaining control.

"I wanted to tell Clara I was sorry."

"Sorry for what? For being who you are?"

"For not having been a little bit different." He took two scalding mouthfuls before nonchalantly changing the subject. "What do you think of Clara?"

"I barely know her."

"Really?"

"Since both of you looked lost that evening, I introduced you to her."

"I can't find her number. Could you give it to me?"

"I don't have it," said Faustine. "She's Maud's friend. She's the one who called to tell me you were breaking up."

That wasn't good news. Maud had been wanting to sleep with Virgil for years. Resisting her took a certain self-control (yoga helped a lot) since she had silky hair, a body to die for, and a talent for sarcasm. As soon as he left Faustine's, he called Maud and left a message on her answering machine saying that he urgently wanted to see her.

Once Virgil had gotten home, because night had fallen, he put on the cave explorer's helmet and lit its light so that he could move around in his apartment. Faustine had given him a box that Salome had dropped off for him at her place.

Salome was Virgil's last girlfriend, and he didn't know why she'd left him. She'd called him to tell him it was over, but the neighbor above and the one next to him had been putting so much heart into simulating orgasm that he hadn't heard the explanations. He hadn't dared ask her to repeat herself. He was a fatalist, and was sure that she had very good reasons. Their affair had lasted several months and ended at the beginning of summer. Salome hated Virgil's neighborhood, so he would come to her apartment in the Gobelins, right next to place d'Italie. He'd left shirts, pants, underwear, records, and books there. He certainly didn't mind getting them back.

He opened the box. This wasn't his stuff. The shirts belonged to a man who was twice his size and whose taste was also twice as bad. He hated novelty shirts. The pants belonged in the same category. Salome had mistaken the clothes of another boyfriend for his. Did she know him that poorly? Did she think he could have worn threads like that? It pissed him off. The records were just as bad. It wasn't the kind of music he listened to. Everything he'd told Salome, everything they'd given each other had been forgotten. Sometimes he'd think about her, about their good times, their improvised dinners on the banks of the Seine, the movies they saw at the theater on rue Champollion. Now, all at once, those memories lost their meaning.

In the trash he found a menu from a Japanese deli and ordered a selection of sushi, sashimi, and *maki*. He was preparing for a Wednesday evening alone, depressed. He retightened the strap of his cave explorer's helmet, poured himself a glass of wine, and started to think about his love life.

The light from the cave explorer's helmet pierced the glass of wine, bathing the wall in red. Virgil took a sip.

He'd never kept in contact with his old involvements. Not because the separations had been painful, but because they hadn't been painful enough.

There's a disturbing parallel between the development of tourism and an increase in the number of love affairs. We love like we travel, for short periods and in organized excursions. We fall in love for the souvenirs of

the experience, for the letters and the collection of sensations, so that we can treat our irises to new colors; or talk
about it at the office, to our friends and to our shrink.
There isn't any difference between love and travel: we
always come back.

Why had he fallen in love with these women? They
were all attractive and intelligent, but they lacked personality. Their main quality lay in the fact that he wasn't
suffering very much from not seeing them. Maybe he'd
chosen them for that; he'd fallen in love with women
whose loss wouldn't cause him any lasting pain. Nothing
could happen between them. At least nobody had been
hurt.

Before the appearance/disappearance of Clara, there
had been no surprises in his life. It was an ordinary life,
but a controlled one. He'd achieved stability.

Virgil knew that he'd lacked ambition. There's a difference between being ambitious and really putting yourself into what you're doing. From now on, he swore, he'd
be as exacting with his personal life as with his work; he'd
correct himself constantly, wouldn't be afraid to toss away
rough copies of himself. But was trying to find a woman
whom he'd never been with proof of ambition or of mental
imbalance? He wasn't certain of the answer to that.

The doorbell rang. It was the Japanese food. Virgil
paid, drained his glass, left his apartment. He gave the

sushi to the hookers who were on the stroll and headed for the place de la République.

The rain was refreshing. He was surprised that his hair wasn't getting wet, and realized that he'd kept on the cave explorer's helmet.

Soon the sign for the Monoprix at rue du Temple appeared. Its red letters glistened in the twilight. Virgil already felt better. When he went through the automatic doors and entered the light, the pressure on his shoulders disappeared. There is no better viaticum or diversion than consumption. On some lonely nights, when socializing seemed devoid of sense, when he no longer had any faith in evenings with friends, a stroll through the rows of the Monoprix warmed his heart. He could never get over being allowed to buy these wonders. He'd rediscover products from his childhood like so many teddy bears and security blankets: a cereal brand, an orange box of powdered chocolate, detergent with a surprise inside, a bottle of mineral water. The product hadn't changed. This was what remained of the past, what had survived without a scratch, this was where he could pour out his feelings. Unfortunately, marketing departments were changing the shape and color of packages more and more often.

Virgil took a basket near the checkout lines. The security guard studied him with suspicion, pointed at his helmet and leaned down to whisper something into the ear of his superior; he followed Virgil for a moment. Virgil meandered to the fruit-and-vegetable section, past the dairy products, the alcoholic beverages, the juices, and beauty products. Their colors reminded him of fields of flowers. He only needed to look at a product to be transported to where it had come from, to think of the peasants who'd planted seeds, harvested the fruit, processed the food.

Virgil saw similarities between the supermarkets and the banks of the Ganges in Benares. The escalators leading to the food department were like ghats, those staircases that the Hindus used to go down to bathe in the purifying river. We flock to a supermarket like the Hindus to their sacred river: to take advantage of its anti-anxiety and dietary curative powers.

Shopping offered a chance to share a collective mystical experience. Side by side we all walk. Each carries his basket, pushes his cart. No one hides what he buys. You know who has sensitive skin, who loves andouillette sausage, and who has children who like chocolate cereals with animal shapes. You know which woman loves lemon meringue tarts, has dry hair; and that single portion of salmon with curried rice means she's single.

Shopping baskets make known our intimacy; we know everything about one another's bathrooms, toilets, the contents of our fridges, and the makeup of our families. Innocent exhibition is the rule. We're naked as a tiny tot, and it doesn't bother us.

From a truck parked across the bicycle lane on boulevard Magenta, four men were unloading dozens of wedding dresses on hangers, wrapped inside transparent plastic dry-cleaner dustcovers. Virgil and Armelle were sitting at la Taverne, near the Gare de l'Est. It was just about three hundred feet from the Gare du Nord; but unlike its big sister, it was unpleasant and unsightly, the area around it less hospitable.

Armelle had decided to begin her weekend early on this Thursday and join Anne-Élisabeth in Strasbourg, taking the first train. Her luggage, a smart-looking leather bag, was lying on the seat next to her. Since she'd opened her office, Armelle had bought two beautiful items for herself: this travel bag and the lace-up boots that she had on today. She was dressed in a navy blue suit. Her pulled-back hair brought out her face. Her scented skin gave off a delicate blend of tuberose and spices.

The waiter brought a basket of croissants, two orange juices, a coffee, and a decaf. A fine drizzle blended with the last traces of night.

Still filled with drowsiness, Virgil touched his decaf to his lips. He seemed to spend his time drinking. His entire social life depended on drinks. Every time he was having a conversation, he was drinking (wine, tea, herbal tea, soda, decaf). As if he drank to moisten and lubricate words that were, at times, badly hewn or deliberately rough. Armelle cut a croissant in two. She bit into a pointed end and left the rest. She took a swallow of orange juice. Virgil took the piece of croissant left behind by his friend. They were a little over thirty, and the pounds were accumulating quickly. Virgil had left behind his usual breakfast of oatmeal and soy milk a moment ago. His legs felt heavier and his belly a little fatter. A light breeze had come up; he pulled the collar of his jacket around his neck.

"I think the origin of the problem of my love life has to do with the fact that I haven't had any positive models."

"Your parents are a very nice couple," said Armelle.

Virgil's parents liked Armelle a lot. Every time they came to Paris they had dinner with her. They thought of her as their own daughter.

"My father flings knives at my mother," said Virgil. "Is that your idea of a stable couple?"

"It's a circus act."

"An unconscious attempt at murder."

"That's your interpretation. The important thing is that your parents are happy."

"My life would have been simpler if they'd been a little less happy and a little more normal."

This morning he'd risen in a bad mood. He hadn't had enough sleep, and, from the little he understood, his life seemed miserable to him. Armelle told him that everything wasn't that dark, and he cursed her for spoiling his depression. He subscribed to the negative image of his childhood; he'd constructed himself according to it. It was agonizing for him to admit that he hadn't been immersed in an environment as toxic as he claimed. Obviously, everything hadn't been roses; he'd had no security, stability, normality, creature comforts. He'd lived in unhealthy places; the circus smelled of dung, mold, and damp tarpaulin. But his parents were a resourceful couple. It had taken him until now to discover that he'd inherited that strength from them. The treasure was right there staring him in the face, and he hadn't seen it. When he thought of his parents, he saw them laughing. It was the first image that came into his mind.

"I could have been a model for you, too," said Armelle, determined to tear him away from his brooding.

"You only see your girlfriend once a week. You don't live together."

"Have I violated international law? Your head's full of idiotic, petrified principles."

The discussion was taking a turn that Virgil didn't like. Armelle had seized control of it.

"Your train's going to leave," he said, looking at the time on his cell phone.

Even if it was out of the question to show it, he was curious about what she had to say.

"As I see it, if your love affairs have all been failures," stated Armelle without paying attention to his remark, "it's because you loved those women for one reason: in the hope of having a normal life."

After glancing at the check, Virgil dug into his pocket; he put a bill under his saucer. Of course she was right, but he wasn't planning on recognizing it today.

His friend was removing a bandage from an old wound that had scarred over. He was attached to this bandage; he couldn't remember living without it. In life, we navigate between the pain that people cause us and the suffering we cause ourselves. One day we come to the realization that they're the same.

"There's another problem," said Armelle.

Virgil closed his eyes, as if the visual eclipse of his friend could protect him from what she was about to say to him.

"You're jealous."

"Not in the slightest," he said, a little too quickly.

"Then why haven't you ever asked to meet Anne-Élisabeth?"

"I was jealous. I admit it."

Virgil was twitching with pleasure and pride.

"We have a great friendship," Armelle went on, "but we'll never be together. We're an asexual, autarkic couple."

"In other words, a happy couple."

The moment he pronounced those words, Virgil understood that nothing could have been truer, but that this was a problem. Luckily, Dr. Zetkin was coming back in two weeks.

"I want you to want to know the woman I love," said Armelle.

"And do you want to meet Clara?"

"If you manage to prove she exists, I'd be delighted to."

The tension in the conversation eased up. A long silence followed. The two friends were moved by these revelations.

A truck parked in front of the large florist's on the corner of the boulevard. The flowers were tied together in lots. They looked like hundreds of lovely prisoners held tight by their shackles. Virgil got up from the table and went to find the florist. He handed him a bill and left with a bouquet of sunflowers. He liked the lack of proportion between their heads and their bodies, their awkwardness, and the cheerful simplicity of their big yellow petals.

"For Anne-Élisabeth," he said, holding out the bouquet to Armelle.

"That's sweet," she answered, "you're an angel. We could go to dinner, the three of us."

You're magnificent, thought Virgil in reaction to what his friend had just said. Her intelligence literally shone on her face.

"Let's not go too fast," he said.

Armelle placed her tarot deck on the table and pushed it toward Virgil. He had the feeling that he could let himself go—get into the fantasy of a fortune-telling session. He took a card. Just when he wanted to turn it over, Armelle put it back in the deck.

"I can't see what card I took?"

"You're too impatient."

Armelle had the power to stop time. She put the conversation on hold and looked at her companion with her amazing eyes, a smile on her lips. You never knew if she was thinking or giving a chance to the other person to collect his wits. During that pause, it occurred to Virgil that they were fraternal twins. They knew each other so well. He could count on her as much as he could count on himself. Armelle was his only terra firma.

"I'm not sure that it's a good idea to look for Clara," she finally said. "You ought to concern yourself with discovering why you don't remember her, and not why she acted as she did. The real mystery is your amnesia. How did it happen that you forgot about the meeting with her at that party?"

"I'd been drinking."

"Three glasses of punch."

Armelle wasn't giving him any way out. He surrendered.

"I know. It's not enough to explain the hole, that gap in my memory."

Trying to put his finger on the reason for this disturbing phenomenon was good advice. It wasn't necessary, and obviously not a good idea, to run after Clara. Armelle was a sensible sibyl. Virgil remembered that Orpheus loses the woman he loves because he's in a hurry to find her. He's inconsolable and rejects all women. He ends up torn to pieces by the maenads. But Clara wasn't Eurydice; she wasn't passive and wasn't waiting for him to save her.

Armelle got up, the bouquet of flowers in her hand. Virgil carried her bag. They walked into the station.

Armelle's train was listed on the departure panel. Virgil went with her all the way to her car. There was something tender and natural about the way they kissed goodbye spontaneously. No, they weren't like brother and sister, but like two young cats.

**Virgil headed for** boulevard de Magenta. He had the time to stop back at his place before meeting Maud. He'd insisted upon their seeing each other that morning. He'd taken the day off.

He remembered that his father had instilled one crucial thing in him: the importance of having good shoes. He'd advised him that, as soon as he had money, he should buy some (English, if possible), ones that would hold up, which he could count on and wouldn't wear out; because with good shoes you can walk, you have your place on the ground ("They're a house for your feet," he'd say); and walking helped you think; so—concluded his father—if you want good ideas, choose good shoes.

At the corner of the boulevard and rue du Faubourg-Saint-Denis, Virgil got a to-go cup of tea from a bakery. He didn't put the tea bag in the cup, and took a swallow of hot water.

When he got home, he found a postcard from his parents. The circus was stationed in Provins. He was moved by their simple words, written on the back of a photo of the Tour César ("an octagonal donjon with a square base dating from the twelfth century," said the caption). He opened a large drawer in the closet and put the postcard in the album where he kept all of them.

Above the couch, a corner of the poster for the circus had become unstuck. Virgil climbed on the armrest and put a piece of Scotch tape on it. On the red and gold poster were acrobats, stars, and a big top. An elephant was balanced on a wire like a tightrope walker.

For a certain number of women, Virgil was only attractive when he was suffering from an unhappy love affair. It happened often, so the most fantastically neurotic women found him very much to their liking. Maud took the cake in that category.

The young woman had tried to have them meet in her apartment, with its view of the Parc des Buttes-Chaumont. Virgil, who'd already seen the place during some parties in the past, remembered the gigantic, welcoming bed, the charming décor, her miniature Buddhist temple, the colonial fan, the bouquet of lavender in the window of the kitchen. He was awed by the colors and scents in the bathroom: the witch hazel, rose, and shea butter creams; the quince soap and clay shampoo; the many little vials with natural essences; the horse-chestnut bubble bath, berry candle, and the cotton discs hanging at the mirror. He would have liked to remain for hours in that bathroom that was so clean, well-lit, soothing. Maud's apartment was a love trap. Virgil insisted that they meet in a café bordering the Jardin du Luxembourg.

An obvious sign of Virgil's lack of composure was his arriving early for meetings (whether friendly, romantic, medical, or professional). Punctuality was like a red line he never crossed; the thought of not being present at the moment when he'd said he would be made him anxious, as if lateness, even to the smallest degree, revealed not only a simple fault, but real betrayal. For some time, he'd been committed to a major reform of himself that was supposed to lead to more serenity, and he'd been training himself to cut down on the tendency to arrive early; in the near future, he hoped, he'd achieve appropriate, inconsequential lateness.

At least there was some advantage to his neurosis; getting there early allowed him to become familiar with the café and locate the emergency exit. He sat down at a table far enough from the bar to avoid an argument going on between the manager and a customer, and he ordered a green tea.

The middle of the morning on a weekday is the best time to take advantage of the simple pleasure of sitting in a café. The décor recalled a medieval dining room. A set of armor kept watch over the entrance, a red drapery led to the kitchen, a sofa sat opposite the large fireplace. Virgil took notes on a paper napkin, going over what he'd say and how he'd get Clara's phone number.

Every time he was supposed to meet someone, it

became a source of anxiety. He'd spend hours preparing, warming up, and finding topics for discussion. Unfortunately, his monotonous life didn't offer many opportunities for conversation. Virgil was convinced that human beings went out together, got married, bought new electronic gadgets, and had children for the sole purpose of having something to talk about when they were alone together. Deep down, Virgil was especially fond of talking about conversation itself, about its freedoms and its limits. He also liked to keep quiet and observe what the person opposite him did with his silence; if she treated it with care or if she hurried to tear it to shreds.

Every male eye in the café was glued to Maud when she walked in. She was wearing a tartan skirt and black knee-length stockings, high heels, and a dark green V-necked sweater; her hair, carelessly pinned back, fell onto her shoulders. Pages stopped turning, espresso spoons froze in midair, time stopped. Maud's perfume came between Virgil and his reflections. They kissed and did the usual initial catching up. Maud took in the boy's expression and ordered an *orange pressée*.

Virgil didn't broach the subject of Clara immediately, to avoid giving Maud the impression that he was using her. He also wanted to purge her of the insane idea she had of going to bed with him. To discourage women who came on to him, Virgil had mastered two speeches that had a radical effect. The first was entitled "There are four species of pigeons in Paris and not one, as is usually thought." At the end of that dissertation, no woman had ever asked for his phone number. For Maud, he'd decided to use his second speech, the one on programmed cell death. He took a sip of tea and talked to her about this fascinating phenomenon: the cells of our body are continually committing suicide. As soon as they're no longer capable of doing this, we die.

"Which means, and I know it's paradoxical," concluded Virgil, "that suicide is peculiar to life."

"You called me to talk about biology?" she said, as she leaned closer to him.

Virgil caught sight of her gold pendant in the form of a heart; then his eyes discovered the entirety of Maudian beauty. It was ridiculous, but he knew that sleeping with Maud would amount to cheating on Clara. They hadn't been together, he should have been free, yet he knew that if he slept with another woman, he'd be unfaithful. He was committed to this unknown woman. He thought about Ulysses and the ordeals and temptations he endured before finding Penelope. Despite Maud's breasts, lips, eyes, neck, he had no intention of succumbing. What is more, if he slept with her, it would be disappointing, because it takes time to feel comfortable with the body of someone else. He was too much of a perfectionist to be satisfied with fooling around with a person he didn't know.

"You do know her," Armelle had argued one day while they were shopping at the market at Barbès, under the elevated subway. "You've known her for years."

"I don't know her emotionally."

"It's entirely your job to get to know her better."

Virgil thought about it a lot and weighed the pros and cons. He'd ended up figuring that the only hindrance to getting it on with Maud was her great beauty. Maud was a love goddess, a treasury of sensuality, an invitation to luxury. There was something insane about a woman as magnificent as that setting her heart on him. He hadn't slept with her for the same reason that he didn't go to the top restaurants or wear clothes from the trendy stores: she was too good for him. For the first time, he saw how anachronistic this point of view was. He was no longer the poor kid in a decrepit circus rattling around from town to town. Not having sex with Maud was an aberration. This beautiful, intelligent woman had been stalking him for years. Out of romanticism, prudishness, or puritanism, he hadn't responded to her advances. Now he regretted letting the opportunity to experience the softness of her skin slip through his hands. He fantasized about the way they would have touched each other; he imagined undressing her, kissing her, caressing her.

Making love with Maud would have been possible on several occasions (at the end of a dinner with friends at her place, when she'd suggested he stay and see her collection of old films; after fireworks on the Fourteenth of July, when they'd ended up lost in Paris and had almost taken a hotel room together; during a relaxing massage session with calendula oil). But Virgil had never found the opportunity to sleep with her enough reason to do so. It was the opposite: the ease with which he could have gone to bed with Maud repulsed him. Virgil needed to be broken in; he needed to believe that the women whom he lusted after didn't want to sleep with him at first, but just to talk, go to an exhibition at a gallery, and discuss a film. Sex was the dessert for a meal of several courses. This attitude did away with the women who were in the most hurry and the least persistent, or the ones who interpreted his distance as disinterest.

Of course, he knew that the only reason he regretted not having slept with Maud was because he would stop himself from doing it from now on. It was typical of the way he functioned. All the same, the two of them didn't have much in common. Even if they ran into each other regularly, they weren't close friends; Maud spent her time partying, drinking, dancing, and taking all sorts of hallucinogens. He liked having a drink with her from time to time, but that was all.

"So you're still working in advertising?" said Maud.

She knew the answer; she was trying to pull Virgil away from his reflections by leading him onto familiar ground.

Virgil felt no shame about practicing his profession, but it seemed as if he were making a confession when he answered. Maud wasn't in any position to get moralistic with him; she was a veterinarian in a large pharmaceutical laboratory and spent her days putting electric wires under the eyelids of chimpanzees, forcing them to gulp down prototypes of drugs for meningitis, hemorrhoids, and shingles. There's a great hypocrisy about those who criticize the field of advertising, because, like everyone with personal and professional dealings, they use the same tools to trick and fascinate, to charm and win over. Advertising is at the basis of human relations; we're constantly doing our own publicity.

"Don't take this wrong, but you're somebody with ideas, it's a pity to make use of them for *that*."

She emphasized the word *that* to make it very clear to him how inappropriate his occupation was. This was a woman who tortured animals and spent her Saturday nights gobbling Ecstasy and champagne, and she thought she could teach him a lesson. Virgil knew that she meant well; like most of his friends, she didn't understand why he worked at Svengali. It didn't match her idea of him.

"I might be stopping," he said.

He kept himself from revealing the reason for the conflict between him and management at the agency. Maud wasn't the only one who talked to him about leaving his job. But to do what? Armelle thought he'd write great stories. He had imagination and style; he wouldn't have any problem writing for television, film, or the theater. He'd have to make a decision soon: stay at Svengali or find something else to do with his life.

Maud wanted to understand why it had ended with Clara. For Virgil this was a chance to get rid of the troublesome flirtation between them, once and for all. After the age of thirty, romantic rendezvous seem like employment interviews. You've had enough bad experiences and you behave cautiously. For once, you don't want to make a mistake, so you ask questions, investigate, interpret the slightest signal in a worrisome way. You know what you're looking for, you're out shopping, and don't hesitate at rejecting the bad apples. Virgil was getting ready to come up with a horrifying depiction of himself. He got a real kick out of playing against established romantic codes.

"What were you like with her?" asked Maud, her chin resting on her crossed hands; she was expecting him to talk about love.

"Ill at ease," said Virgil. "Being in a couple wears me out. It takes too much effort."

Maud was surprised. She knitted her brow and stared at him as if he'd turned into a fat cockroach with little concern for hygiene. She fooled with her straw between her tongue and her teeth, then questioned him about their sex life.

"To be honest," said Virgil, lowering his voice, "it was a real drag for me. And she found me unbearable."

"In my opinion," answered Maud, hoping to keep the positive image of Virgil that she had, "she didn't know how to handle it."

"It's really all my fault. I was wretched."

Maud didn't hide her disappointment. Virgil figured that it would be enough to cool her off. After having given his small donation to the conversation and making a certain number of revelations, he assumed he had the right to ask for some information about Clara.

"Have you known her for a long time?"

"She's Quentin's sister. Do you know Quentin?"

"No."

"He's my boyfriend. About ten days ago, she asked him to tell me that she was leaving you, and I told Faustine. There you are. I'm only an innocent messenger."

Maud was in love. Virgil was wrong. He sat up straight and ordered a glass of wine; he could let the alcohol loosen his inhibitions without worrying about ending up at a hotel. The cataclysmic portrait of himself he'd just produced risked following him for a long time; Maud wasn't the type to keep gossip to herself.

"I thought you were trying to seduce me," said Virgil.

Maud smiled at him as she bit her bottom lip, as if she had been caught doing an adorably stupid and inconsequential prank. "I've always known there wasn't any risk," she admitted. "You were like a friend who was gay, but heterosexual."

"You don't want to go to bed with me?"

"Sorry."

Virgil thought of all the time he'd thought she was coming on to him. He felt like an immature little pup. It was humiliating. Maud's supposed harassment had given him confidence. From now on he'd feel as desirable as a manatee. He was even more pathetic than he'd thought he was. The waiter put the glass of wine down in front of him at the right moment. He needed it. After two good gulps, he continued his investigation.

"What do you think of her?"

"I don't know her very well. I'm interested in her brother; the rest of the world barely exists. My brain's swimming in endorphins."

"Do you like her hair color?" Virgil threw out.

If he gleaned some physical details, even minor ones, the ghost of Clara would gain a bit of embodiment. But Maud wasn't playing that game.

"I never thought about it. While you were together, didn't she say anything about what Quentin thought of me?"

Her eyes were burning. This was a new affair. Maud was obsessed with Quentin.

"We didn't talk about you, or her brother," said Virgil.

He didn't know her last name, her address, or her telephone number. Clara was within hand's reach, but unattainable, the way things are in those dreams when you're trying to catch hold of something without ever managing to.

"And what does this fabulous Quentin do for a living?" he said ruefully.

"He writes children's books."

She listed five titles and the name of a publishing house. They discussed this and that. Maud talked about Quentin, about his wanting to move in and have children, and Virgil talked about his possible job change. They said good-bye.

Virgil walked down boulevard Saint-Michel and turned onto the rue Racine, until he came to a bookstore.

The bookstore found Quentin's last name based on his book titles. All he needed to do now was look up Clara's address in the phone book. As for knowing what he'd say when he was in front of her, Virgil had no idea, and he preferred not to think about it.

Virgil found number 9 on boulevard Pereire. The numeral had been engraved above an imposing woodwork door with studded panels. The architect had left his name on the building under a grotesque figure in the form of a lion's head hewn into the stone. Someone on the fourth floor with the window open was practicing a piece from Bartók's *For Children*. In tune with Baron Haussman style, the few pedestrians wore tasteful clothing, their hair nicely arranged and their posture erect, their jaws slightly raised. When he'd first arrived in Paris, Virgil had loved the hustle and bustle, the crowds, the café terraces, the musicians in the subway. But gradually he'd developed a taste for the quiet of wide, deserted streets, where there was no risk of running into one of his friends or somebody he'd want to be friends with.

This day off was coming at just the right moment. Virgil felt as if he were playing hooky.

A stooped concierge with a long white beard told Virgil that Clara had moved. What's more, the apartment was for rent; would he like to see it? It was on the fourth floor,

Virgil's favorite: high enough to avoid the noise of traffic, low enough to protect against vertigo.

So, Clara had escaped again, as if being elusive were part of her identity. Virgil thought of a greyhound race course and that fake rabbit attached to the tracks to goad agitated dogs into racing to the finish line. He wondered whether Clara was a lure forcing him to act and think.

Her having moved frustrated him and soothed him at the same time. He was disappointed about not uncovering the figure who'd plotted this farce. But he was also relieved that the story wasn't over, that she'd kept her dynamic nature and her secret. He sensed intuitively that it was too soon to close the book; he wanted the adventure to go on. Actually, he was realizing that he was afraid to find her, afraid of being disappointed, or afraid of disappointing her.

The apartment was empty; all the furniture was gone, and it had been meticulously cleaned. It was like the perfect crime scene: no body, no clues, and certainly no fingerprints. White rectangles on the gray walls revealed the past presence of paintings and posters. Two little round holes patched with Spackle indicated where the shelves had been. Virgil studied the marks in the floor left by the feet of the bed, the shadow of a chest of drawers against one wall, the dusty outline of a mirror. They were like photographic negatives that made it possible to reconstitute the exact order of the things that had been in the apartment. He sniffed every corner of the bathroom in search of any vestiges of Clara's fragrance, shampoo, or nail polish, but the place had been washed with bleach and aired out; Virgil's olfactory cells were left as hungry as they'd been before.

He was surprised. He'd imagined that she lived somewhere that was more politically correct. In fact, he'd never been in love with any girl who lived in such a bourgeois neighborhood. He didn't even have friends who lived in one. It was another world. How could a person younger than sixty have been able to live here? Maybe the apartment belonged to her grandmother in the provinces; maybe she had a roommate; maybe she was so sensitive that she couldn't stand noise and crowds. He was happy that she wasn't like the woman he could have imagined. She was thwarting clichés and prejudices. He liked that.

"How was the tenant?"

Grumbling because of the time Virgil was making him lose, the concierge explained to him that he took care of three buildings, each of them with about twenty apartments, with families that were sometimes large. More than a hundred people lived here; he was most likely to know the ones who caused problems.

"The ones who have big dogs and play their music too loud," he said more specifically.

Muttering, the concierge handed him the keys and went back downstairs. Virgil stayed for a moment to walk around the apartment. He took a breath of air and kept it prisoner inside his lungs, the way he would have done with hashish to get the full effect. He lay down at the place where the bed had been, rolled sideways, and mimed taking someone in his arms; he pressed the invisible being against him tenderly but forcefully. He opened the mouth and slid his tongue over the edges of her teeth. An intense, radiating warmth coiled through his body, as if the invisible person that he was holding in his arms had come alive; he trembled and noticed that he was getting hard. The discovery of his erection pulled him out of his fantasy.

Drained and discouraged, Virgil went home and collapsed onto the couch. He put some batteries in his clock radio. The tinny, familiar voices put his mind at rest. The newscasters set the wheels of the information factory spinning; they brought him the weather, but the only value in their words was prophylactic. According to Armelle, journalists, market research companies, and politicians used systems of thought and speech borrowed from divination and magic. Economic commentaries are no more than predictions and prayers seeking to be answered. Virgil closed his eyes; he saw them behind their mikes, wearing the pointed hats of sorcerers and magic rings. He emptied the rest of the bottle of wine into a glass. There was nothing else to drink, nothing to eat. The apartment seemed abandoned.

Armelle must have been in the arms of Anne-Élisabeth. He imagined them walking on the Mimram Bridge between France and Germany or down a row of the botanical garden. The thought brought serenity, lulled him. He jiggled the wine in his glass.

A key turned in the lock of the entrance door. Panicking, Virgil got off the couch, spilling the wine onto the floor. A man in a suit with a bunch of keys in his hand entered; two women with showy manes of hair were behind him, talking and smoking. Their surprise at finding him in the middle of the living room and the fact that they kept cool was reassuring. These weren't burglars.

"What are you doing here?" asked Virgil.

"Showing the apartment," answered the man, swinging the keys between his fingers back and forth; he skirted the puddle of wine on the floor.

"There has to be a mistake."

The two women wandered through the apartment. They took stock of the premises, ran a hand over the wallpaper, looked at the cracks in the ceiling, the workmanship of the double-paned windows, the state of the floor, the pipes. The man was certain about his right to invade a private space. He wasn't the slightest bit uncomfortable. Virgil felt ill at ease, as if he'd been reduced to nothing. One of the women screamed when she opened the fridge. Virgil still hadn't emptied it. The odor of things decomposing was horrible.

"The previous tenant's dead," whispered the man in a way that would keep him from being heard by the two women.

"I'm not," said Virgil. "I made a mistake."

There was a moment of surprise, but it didn't last.

The realtor was preoccupied with renting the apartment and pocketing his commission, the rest wasn't very important.

"That doesn't change anything," he said, "the lease has been canceled."

Virgil had forgotten to inform the owner of his "miraculous recovery" and to ask him not to take into account the letter he'd sent ending his lease. The realtor shoved aside the fruit basket on the table, opened his briefcase there, and took out a sheet of paper.

"Here's my authorization for going ahead with the rental," he said, handing the paper to Virgil. "You have two months to move out."

"Shit."

The two women were satisfied with their visit. Although they'd tried to camouflage it under their conservative clothing, Virgil knew they were hookers. They'd agreed to rent the apartment for a fortune. The intruders left. Virgil called the owner, but in vain; he wouldn't renege on the canceled lease. For a moment Virgil considered taking Clara's apartment. But that would add to his confusion, and the next step would doubtlessly be a psychiatric hospital. He was going to have to begin looking for a new place.

\* \* \*

The sun had set. Virgil groped around for the cave explorer's helmet. He lit the lamp at the front. His head was killing him; he blew his nose. Wilhem Fliess, one of Freud's great platonic passions, thought that men, like women, had their own cycles; their "periods" were characterized by headaches and runny noses. It was a hypothesis that didn't seem unreasonable to Virgil.

He curled up on the couch to think about Clara, the only thing exciting and real about his existence. He made an effort to plunge into the memory of the evening they met. He saw the building on rue Pernety near the post office, the grocery where he bought a bottle of wine, Maud with her elbows on the kitchen window and a half-liter can of beer in her hand, Nadia dancing with her fiancé to *Como dizia o poeta*, the clean faces of people he didn't know, the haze of cigarette smoke, feet stepping on his. But his memory could only make out the shadow of Clara in all the hubbub. He saw her talking to several people, serving herself a glass of punch, and borrowing a cigarette from Faustine. But as soon as he entered the room where he'd met Clara, a light filled the doorway and blinded him.

Maybe his brain wanted to keep these few minutes hidden inside to protect them; maybe he wanted to prevent this memory from having to confront the violence of the world, to keep it a secret forever.

He walked past the Gare du Nord. As if he were leafing through an exhaustive catalog of femininity, he examined every woman he passed: brunettes, blondes,
redheads; women in suits, jeans, a hat, veil, or scarf, or
with purses in various styles; wearing leather boots, san-
dals, sneakers. A lot of them wore perfume, and most
were subtly made up with eyes that were blue, green,
gray, brown, or multicolored, shielded by glasses or contacts. They came in every size and every age. Virgil was
hoping that some detail would awaken his memory of
Clara. But the faces didn't kindle anything in him.

He couldn't picture Clara; and strangely, other
women were beginning to lose their reality. He wasn't
turning around anymore when they went by; he no longer
valued their shapes, gestures, the way their hair moved.
Even the women he'd been in love with weren't as close
to him as this Clara, a woman he didn't know. Her invisible face was less out of focus than those of his former
lovers. He'd kissed too many women whose very words
and feelings were out of focus. Clara's invisibility had
more meaning and consistency than the other women's
visibility.

Virgil had believed that memory was a function; now
he realized that it was an action. There were so many
things that he hadn't taken in, as if he'd snipped at reality with scissors to give it a shape that suited him. It had

been an effective way of making the world comfortable, a way of justifying his choices.

Forgetting his meeting with Clara wasn't the most outrageous thing he'd done; it was memorizing everything else around it, the party and those uninteresting people. The symptom was obvious: he'd suppressed the only interesting thing there was to see in order to preserve the details of a world and a life that had no importance, that left him cold.

Suddenly dizzy, he sat down on a bench along the boulevard. He hadn't eaten since breakfast with Armelle. He raised his hand to signal a taxi. A few minutes later, he was sitting at a table at Pho Dong Hu'o'ng and ordering noodle soup.

When Virgil got to Svengali's offices Friday morning, the receptionist handed him an envelope. A letter printed on thick beige paper admonished him in a paternalistically benevolent tone to accept the promotion and the raise in salary. The letter's author, the director of human resources, had blended compliments about the work he'd accomplished with thinly veiled threats about what would happen if he refused. He reminded Virgil that he'd given him his first job—in spite of his lack of experience and diplomas.

Virgil didn't know what he would have done without Svengali (not much of an optimist, he imagined being a cashier, a salesclerk, a cleanup man), but having someone talk about him being indebted irked him to the highest degree. They were trying to put pressure on him by exploiting the gratitude and esteem he felt for Svengali and its directors. He tore up the letter and walked into the elevator.

He was in a hurry to take refuge in his work, in that wonderful world of effort rewarded. Work gave him access to a state of weightlessness, a body with no mass for which death no longer existed; he controlled the universe.

Figuring he'd make the most of the quiet, solitude, and his cartons of yogurt, Virgil walked into the Idea Room. But the six chairs around the table were occupied by interns and some of the new guard of young employees. The only place available was at one end of the table. Every face turned toward him. A swarm of "hellos" descended upon him. A tall, thin intern handed him a glass of water. Apparently someone had called a meeting that he was in charge of running. Management—Simone, perhaps—was trying to force his hand and foist his position on him. Virgil clamped the back of the chair with his fingers and tried to speak, but then sighed and left the room. Simone stuck her head out of her office. She called out to him, but he didn't answer, and left the building.

His knowledge of unions amounted to almost nothing. Circus performers don't have a union to defend them against police harassment and hostile town councils. If Virgil had wanted to remain faithful to the circus tradition, he would have gone to 33 rue des Vignoles, in the twentieth arrondissement, where the headquarters of the anarchist confederation were located. But in his imagination, the Confédération général du travail, or CGT, was in the best position to lead the fight that was brewing (he remembered articles about its strongmen not hesitating to use crowbars, bolts, and ball bearings against employers and their goons). Virgil realized that it amounted to a consumer choosing an established brand: their red acronym was the incarnate archetype of a French labor union.

The union offices were located at the beginning of boulevard de la Villette. The gray, angular building with its unadorned façade had been dreamed up by an architect who lacked a limbic system. The interior decoration hadn't changed since the 1970s: orange chairs and an apple green counter, brown linoleum on the floor establishing a startling aesthetic that wasn't devoid of appeal. Virgil went to the reception area. Behind the desk of mauve plywood, three women were answering the telephone and chatting good-humoredly. Virgil explained that he was having a conflict with his employer. They advised him to contact the local chapter of his company. He answered that there wasn't any union representative where he was working. The secretaries looked at him with pity. One of them filled out a card with the information he gave her.

A large wooden sculpture representing the legendary Haymarket Riot in Chicago stood in the middle of the room. As Virgil waited, he leafed through the magazine for the union and its various category-specific incarnations. Even though he'd been nicely received, he was still ill at ease. He felt as if he were doing something taboo; the union had supported the Soviet invasion of Hungary. If his parents and their friends learned about this strategy on his part, it would hurt them. To break free of such distressing thoughts, the young man concentrated on his reading. The magazine told about recent struggles, sit-ins at factories, and victories that had been won. As if reciting a mantra, he kept telling himself that he'd made the right decision by coming here. Thirty-two minutes later, his name was called.

A woman in black velvet pants and a burgundy blouse, with a brooch in the form of a bee pinned to her bosom, asked him to enter her office. She read the file card that succinctly explained Virgil's situation. On the ledge outside the window, red roses in a vase were beginning to lose their petals.

The woman picked up a copy of the work code and a handful of files that were overflowing with papers; she put on her glasses and reassured him that his employer had no choice but to raise his salary; she cited a collective labor agreement and talked about organizing a union chapter at his agency.

"I think you're on the wrong track," interrupted Virgil.

She peered at him over her glasses. Her life was a

succession of meetings with salary workers who were being laid off, harassed, or underpaid; she'd been certain that a quick review of Virgil's file would be enough to grasp the problem. Holding the file with her fingertips, she read it attentively.

"They want to give me a promotion and raise my salary," said Virgil.

The woman's face underwent a change. The expression that said *serious professional* gave way to fatigue. She took off her glasses, collapsed into her chair, and rubbed her face.

"You know, most people would be delighted."

Virgil sensed that she considered him a waste of time and energy. She was controlling herself, to keep from showing him the door.

"Then let them give my raise to most people."

"That's an excellent idea, but I don't think it has any immediate relevance. Whatever the case, the union is not going to help you refuse a raise."

"But I have a right to," said Virgil. He wanted to strike the desk with his fist.

"What planet do you live on? You've got no money problems here, so take advantage of it. Your claim is outrageous."

Virgil ended up back on the sidewalk, feeling sheepish. It was raining. He passed a hand through his wet, oily hair. He pulled up the collar of his jacket and walked to the bus stop.

Since he'd come to Paris, he'd tried to live a normal life that would exorcise the rootlessness and the anxieties of his childhood. He'd done a rather good job of believing and convincing others that he'd been assimilated and wasn't the child of itinerant street acrobats. But the union rep had been right: he was abnormal. His relationships with others, his love affairs, his job, even the place he lived were all part of a life that could only be called peculiar.

The truth was that for years he'd made a desperate effort to attain normality that, down deep, he despised. The mask was coming off, and he didn't regret it.

Saturday at dawn, Virgil woke up to the crashing of doors coming off their hinges and locks being forced. The racket climbed from floor to floor. He woke up completely when the screws in his own door rattled loudly onto the tile floor of the entranceway. Two police officers, a man and a woman, burst into the apartment; the man held a flashlight, the woman a weapon. They were wearing navy blue jackets and armbands.

"Hello," was the only thing Virgil could think to say.

He squinted because of the ray of light pointing at his eyes.

He'd given up trying to understand anything about his life. So having the police materialize in his room didn't faze him. It was just a new weird thing to add to the list.

The policeman grabbed some clothes from the box Salomé had sent and threw them at Virgil, ordering him to get dressed. The young man murmured that those clothes were too big and too bright and didn't belong to him. The policeman gave him a slap on the head. Virgil put on a pair of red pants with silver stars and a loose-fitting shirt with a rainbow on it.

The rhythmic pressure of boots on the stairs and floor made the building quake; the foundations seemed fragile, the walls about to crumble. About forty police officers moved along the corridors and the stairway. They flushed out the prostitutes and their customers and handcuffed them. They responded to any screams or cries of protest with whacks and insults. The motley crowd was divided up into four paddy wagons parked in front of the station. It was early, and there were no passersby; the gates of the shops were lowered, the lights in apartments off. The gigantic statues in front of the station, each representing a major destination of the trains, were the only witnesses to what happened. Brussels, London, Berlin, Warsaw, Amsterdam, and Vienna helplessly watched the sweep. Bums kept sleeping in front of the station.

As they pushed Virgil along, he tried to explain that all this fuss had nothing to do with him. An officer made his handcuffs tighter. In the paddy wagon people were whining, weeping, declaring their innocence. Virgil had no chance of being heard; he gave in and fell back against the shoulder of his fourth-floor neighbor, an African woman wearing a white wig. A man was sobbing in the arms of a transvestite. Everyone was shattered by the violence of the intervention. Most of the prostitutes and their customers were disheveled, barely dressed, wearing a bathrobe, a pair of pants without the belt, shoes without socks, a jacket over bare shoulders. The paddy wagons pulled out. Virgil watched the Gare du Nord disappearing through a window covered with wire mesh. The statues in front seemed to be waving at him.

The sirens of the vehicles weren't on, as if the raid were supposed to be kept secret. The operation must have been important, because they weren't taking them to the district station but to 36 quai des Orfèvres, on the île de la Cité, which is the headquarters of the Detective Division. The large, cobblestoned courtyard contained about a dozen police cars, some unmarked sedans, an ambulance. The day had barely begun, the streetlamps were still shining.

The police opened the paddy wagons. Two groups were formed: on one side were the prostitutes; on the other, the customers. An officer ordered the prostitutes to follow him into a building for cross-examination. Foreigners without papers were going to be deported; the locals would be liable for a fine. When the prostitutes were out of view, a captain spoke to the customers. Apparently it was still less reprehensible to lower your briefs than to open your thighs, because they were told that they were free to leave. They went through the entrance, some of them slowly, others more hurriedly, a hand holding up their pants and their shirts fluttering in the wind.

Virgil remained alone in the middle of the courtyard. Stripped of his companions, he felt naked. The group no longer protected him. The police officers rubbernecked him, making comments about his rainbow shirt, his large pants with the stars, and his dumbfounded expression. A few chuckled.

The sun was rising. It was the first real day of cool autumn weather. Shivers ran through Virgil's body; he sneezed. Gradually the police officers scattered, returning to duty. Virgil rummaged in his pockets but found no sprigs of Lapsang souchong, no tranquilizers. For minutes that felt endless, he stayed like that. He went over his latest yoga lesson and slowed down his breathing. He stretched his chest and chin toward the dark blue sky. The cold was causing spasms in his muscles. His nose was running. He concentrated on counting the windows of the buildings. Then his eyes moved up toward the roofs. He was occupying his mind to keep from slipping into the panic that lay in wait.

Finally, a young lieutenant came to get him. According to the rules, she wore nothing too gaudy: only a little lipstick and some unobtrusive diamond earrings. Contrary to the police who had carried out the raid, her manner wasn't brusque. She led him to a small, empty room, left him under the guard of an officer, and went into an office. For lack of any magazines, Virgil read the recruitment posters for the national police force and the informational messages about drugs and kidnapping. On the walls were Wanted posters with photos. Virgil couldn't resist thinking of them as both effective and caricatured; overexposure, several days of beard growth, and bad hairstyles made them look overdone.

The lieutenant opened the door. Virgil walked in. The desk was composed of two staggered metallic tables; each one had a computer, stacks of paper, cards and photos, and a cup of steaming coffee. The green light at the base of the camera attached to the ceiling indicated that it was recording. The lieutenant pointed him to a chair and switched on her computer. Virgil was shaking from the cold; he was hoping that somebody would bring him coffee or tea, any warm drink at all would do. The lieutenant was typing on her keyboard. She ignored him.

"There has to have been a mistake," said Virgil.

That sentence, he figured, could serve as his motto. It applied to a lot of situations that had occurred in the last two weeks. Maybe even to his entire existence. In a hoarse voice he asked if he was being accused of something. The young lieutenant didn't answer. Virgil expected she was applying tactics of psychological intimidation she'd learned in police school. They weren't going to work with him, though, not now; he was inured to shocks, immune to strategies of destabilization.

"Procuring," said the young women, without moving her eyes away from the computer screen.

"Then it's obvious, there's a misunderstanding."

A man entered. He was wearing a holster and gun. After greeting his colleague by kissing both cheeks, he placed some photos in front of Virgil; they showed him talking with some prostitutes in front of his building. In one photo, a girl was passing him a bill; in another, Virgil was giving condoms to a transvestite.

"I was doing a favor."

"You sure were," said the young female cop. "And the favor you were doing is called pimping."

Virgil carefully explained each photo. Sometimes he did errands for his neighbors, bought them condoms, body lotions, and analgesics. The lieutenant handed him a printout that contained a bank account number.

"And how do you explain the money that you have in the bank?"

Virgil realized what the document was.

"I'm thrifty," he said, flabbergasted.

Everything in his life, he realized, just like in anyone else's, could be interpreted in a criminal light. His behavior (his announced death, canceling his electricity and telephone accounts, as if he were preparing to drop out of sight; his lack of interest in consumption, the reason his bank balance was so high; not to mention his gigantic collection of nudie magazines and photos of Armelle in the raw, hidden under his bed) was particularly liable to suspicion.

"You work in advertising?"

Virgil nodded. In a way, he deserved his arrest; advertising is the world's oldest profession, prostitution is only an adaptation of it. The police weren't really wrong about him. Virgil was surprised to discover that he wasn't unhappy about being arrested. Their intervention was a signal that he had to change.

The police pointed out to him that the use of cocaine was common in his milieu. "That's very possible," answered Virgil. He wasn't interested in what others put into their nostrils, veins, or liver. He had other things to look at. He would have liked to describe the stained-glass windows in certain rooms of the Svengali building, the posters in the hallway, or Simone's office.

"You think I'm selling drugs to my coworkers?"

"We found cocaine in several apartments."

A lot of prostitutes took drugs to cope. The police officer had to be aware of that.

"So I look like a dealer and a pimp to you."

Virgil couldn't help feeling flattered that they were

imagining him in the role of a ballsy, virile dude. An unsociable, irresistible kind of crook, the kind of man who feared nothing and never hesitated to act.

"That's a weird way to dress."

With his bizarre getup and two-day growth of beard, he must have been the spitting image of a pimp as imagined by a young police officer who was into the movies. The only things missing were leather boots, a gold chain, and a pair of shades.

"My life is weird. But everything's okay, isn't it?"

In fact, this episode was of a piece with the madness that had taken over his existence since Clara's message. There was a certain logic to it. Virgil had an urge to give himself up to the whims of the police, to get carried away by the story in their heads, and play a role in it that clashed radically with his real identity. He no longer resembled the person everybody thought he was. He was trying to get rid of his former life.

"Listen," he said, "I'm willing to be the pimp you're looking for. I'm ready to confess."

Maybe this was a sign from fate, a way of leaving the agency and making a fresh start. The fact that this fresh start was beginning with several years of prison was inconvenient, obviously, but he needed a powerful force to wrest him from his overly orderly life. And then, prison is a good school for those who want to change career directions; it would teach you the tricks of the swindler's trade; he'd work out, make contacts.

Of course, the police officers were unsettled by his proposal. They glanced at each other. They'd lost their tense masks and were letting signs of discouragement show, not to mention something like sadness.

"We didn't think you were guilty," said the young woman. "But you're acting strangely."

Apparently that was something that called for questioning and cross-examining. Virgil was no law expert (in college he'd preferred classes in constitutional law to those in the penal category), but he doubted that—for now, anyway—strangeness could be considered an offense or a crime.

"Maybe you noticed something in your building. You've lived there for seven years. We're trying to break up a network."

He'd rubbed shoulders with hookers, talked to them, but he hadn't been preoccupied with the life of his building. He was much too absorbed in his own thoughts to notice anything else at all. If his neighbors had been building a nuclear submarine, he wouldn't have been aware of it. He was sorry about not being able to help these police officers who had gotten up early and insulted, humiliated, and bashed so many people for the noble cause of breaking up a network of prostitution.

All of a sudden, like an epiphany, an idea loomed in his mind: what if he gave Clara's name to the police? He'd tell them he'd seen her prowling around the building, talking to the girls, pocketing some of the profits. He'd describe her as head of the network, dressed in black; he'd talk about a bulge in her jacket that looked like a gun, and about her hardened look. Playing a trick on her would be a way to balance the scales of their relationship. The idea amused him, but of course it wasn't conceivable.

The lieutenant informed him that he'd be held in a cell for twenty-four hours (that was the law, and it would be a shame not to take advantage of it), which was the time needed to verify the source of the money in his savings account. What was more, it would be good of him if he'd submit to a certain number of medical tests. Virgil signed the paper that they handed him and grabbed the cup of coffee on the lieutenant's desk. The liquid was hot. He held it against his cheeks and his entire body shuddered with pleasure.

Two officers went with him to the medicolegal lab on the seventh floor. The room, lit by fluorescent lights, stretched before him for about 150 feet, and the ceiling was very low. The white walls and floor intensified the brightness.

Computers, microscopes, and test tubes had been placed side by side along the three rows through which doctors and biologists moved.

A doctor approached. He was surrounded by three students with notepads in hand, pens poised. They were medical students doing internships. Without introducing himself to Virgil, the doctor stuck a needle into the vein of his arm and withdrew a more-than-negligible amount of blood. He gave the sample to a student. Virgil thought he was gong to conk out; he was sorry he hadn't read the paper carefully before signing an authorization for the tests. The doctor cut one of Virgil's fingernails over a small metal basin. The three students hurried to clip the ones that were left. The doctor lopped off a lock of hair with a surgical knife; Virgil could feel that part of his skull was exposed to the air. The students divided up the lock of hair and put the strands in small plastic bags. While the doctor was scraping the walls of his cheeks with a stick, the students took his fingerprints. Finally, they told him to pee in a cup. The doctor divided the warm yellow liquid among each of the three students' cups.

A police officer led Virgil to the basement. They took a stairway that had been carved into the rock; the walls oozed humidity. Most of the bulbs were blown. Virgil was careful not to miss a step. The prison section of the quai des Orfèvres was made up of a series of cells in the purest tradition of John Haviland's invention for the Eastern State Penitentiary in Philadelphia—meaning that isolation was total. No communication with the other detainees or the guards was possible.

There wasn't a bench in the cell. A small amount of light filtered through a high window. Virgil sat on the concrete floor. In spite of the darkness, he had his first clear vision of his existence, of what he wanted to be and to accomplish.

The next day, at eight in the morning, Armelle was there to meet Virgil when he got out of Detective Division headquarters. She'd cut short her weekend in Strasbourg to pick him up. After a day and a night in jail, Virgil's clothes stuck to his skin and smelled of mildew and urine. The light was blinding; he was squinting. They went back in a taxi. During the trip, Virgil explained the reason for his arrest; Armelle burst out laughing.

She'd made up the guest room. Virgil took a shower. His clothes went into the washing machine. Armelle loaned him an old pair of athletic pants, a black sweatshirt with a hood, and a pair of vivid crimson cashmere socks. Virgil had breakfast in the living room. Armelle had bought some brioches. She gave him a box of *beerawecke* (courtesy of Anne-Élisabeth) and told him about her weekend. At nine, she left him. Her workday was beginning.

Virgil felt liberated, and it had nothing to do with his getting out of prison. He munched on the fruitcake, hung out in the apartment, spent time in front of the partly empty bookshelves, leafed through a tome on botany, the

catalog for an exhibition devoted to Hokusai. Then he
made an important decision: he slipped his copy of *The
Thoughts of the Emperor Marcus Aurelius Antoninus*
into Armelle's bookcase. It was time to get rid of such
impedimenta. After all, he was no Roman emperor;
making it his bible was just a tad exaggerated.

He lay down on the couch, then on his bed, and finally
on Armelle's bed. He picked up the photo on the night
table. It was Anne-Élisabeth. He brought the photo close
to his mouth and blew softly onto it. The face disappeared
under the water vapor. He wiped the surface of the glass
with his sleeve, and Anne-Élisabeth reappeared.

Lazing around an apartment in which the electricity
and the heat functioned was bliss. And it was clear that
someone lived here; there were plants and the fridge was
full.

He opened the window that looked out over the canal
Saint-Martin. The neighborhood suited a quiet life: the
water, the rare presence of cars, the cafés. It was a place
that encouraged meditation. So he tried to reflect upon
his job situation.

A reference came to mind. Antigone was in conflict
with Creon, who had forbidden her to give her brother a
proper burial. The result: she was shut up, died alone.
Myths, tales, literature, art in general all teach that dis-
obedience has its price.

Accepting Svengali's offer would save Virgil from conflict, his world would preserve its homeostasis and his life its ataraxy, which is a state of serene calmness. Human beings obeyed to avoid death. The rule of the good child: if you're good, you'll have good marks, a job, a house, a wife, and neither you nor anyone you love will die. You end up discovering that it's a load of crap, but it sure does work for a helluva long time.

He wasn't going to quit. Not right away. In a little while, he'd go see Simone to accept the promotion and the raise. He'd conform to the plans they had for him for a time. But in secret he'd be preparing his exit. He didn't have enough confidence in himself or in this world to launch into adventure without a security net. Taking risks is the privilege of those who grew up in comfort; the world is made for them. Unconsciously, they know they'll find another situation. Virgil had never had this feeling of self-confidence. That wasn't going to change. The poor, the weak, the sensitive, the exiled have to keep quiet and be cunning.

Virgil watched the people passing by. Thousands of years ago, in the Pliocene Age, elephants must have passed through here. They dipped their trunks into the water, sprayed themselves, washed their little ones, wandered around in groups. Human beings, thought Virgil, are svelte and slender elephants. Human elephants walked by hand in hand, rode skateboards, and ran along the sidewalk. Virgil was overcome with melancholy, because he knew the fate of the elephants. They'd been tamed in order to help out at construction sites, or to be used as weapons, or as vehicles. Above all, they'd been decimated to rob them of their ivory tusks. He wondered what human ivory was, what treasure was part of their nature that justified their annihilation.

During antiquity, elephants almost disappeared. Several species (including the Atlas elephants and those from Syria) died out. The others were saved only by their capacity to fascinate arena audiences, who preferred seeing them do spins or confront gladiators. The elephants moved humans emotionally, and entertained them. And they survived.

In the arena where he had ended up, Virgil was known for both: being entertaining and being moving.

The rue du Faubourg-Saint-Martin was quiet; the lights of the lampposts pushed aside the darkness of the pavement. Families were getting ready for their Sunday evening dinner. A garbage truck turned onto the street with a screeching sound.

Virgil knocked on the door to Clara's brother's apartment. Quentin opened it, a spatula in his hand. The smell of onions and olive oil hovered in the air; the sound of frying floated out from the kitchen. Virgil introduced himself as Clara's ex-boyfriend; he was bringing over some stuff that belonged to her; with his chin, he pointed to the (empty) box under his arm. His heart was beating as never before. He was going to pretend to be one of Clara's old lovers, even though he knew nothing about her. It was risky. Quentin invited him in.

Despite the open window, the smell of food was palpable in the air and in the clothing hanging from a peg. Quentin led him into the kitchen. The apartment was modest; gray walls, lightbulbs without shades. The living room had a convertible couch bed, piles of books, and CDs. Apparently the kitchen was the most important room and the best equipped; it had knives, frying pans, and saucepans; there were spices, condiments, and a basket of fruits and vegetables that were bright and bulging; jars of almonds, walnut halves, pine nuts, and various dried fruits. The shelves were packed with high-quality products; several varieties of oil were lined up on top of the fridge. Grease had stained the wall and ceiling above the gas stove.

"So you're one of Clara's exes," said Quentin, as he stirred the onions in the frying pan.

Virgil nodded. He noticed several joints in a jam jar sitting on the fridge.

"She's coming to dinner tonight," said Quentin. "She should be here in an hour at most. I don't know where you are with all that, but you're welcome to stay. Maud will be here."

The concomitant presence of Maud and Clara promised to be an interesting spectacle. Maud would recount her discussion with Virgil. She'd ask questions about their relationship. Clara was going to be surprised.

"That's nice of you, but I don't think it would be a good idea."

Since Virgil didn't want to dwell on that subject—because the risk of Quentin seeing through his deception was too great—he hurried to change the subject.

"I've read the children's books you write. I really like them."

It was true. He'd liked those strange books.

"They flip me out," claimed Quentin.

He peeled the garlic, removed the hearts of the cloves.

"Children?" said Virgil.

"We never know what they're thinking; they go every way at once and need constant attention."

Quentin took a knife and a wooden cutting board and minced the garlic. By studying the ingredients spread out on the work surface, Virgil came to the conclusion that his host was making lasagna. He opened a can of peeled tomatoes. With a glance, Quentin indicated that he'd appreciate some help; he handed him a pan. Virgil

poured the tomatoes into it. He liked this dish; it stimu-
lated his mind as well as his taste buds. Lasagna was the
result of a world conspiracy: the pasta had been invented
in China, the tomatoes came from America, the onions
from West Africa, the garlic from Egypt (the workers
who built the Great Pyramid of Giza ate enormous quan-
tities of it). Virgil secretly thanked Quentin for having
taken charge of the conversation and leading it onto this
pleasant track. He felt connected, warmed up.

"Then you don't want any children?" asked Virgil.

"No, I do. It's other people's children that I don't like.
I don't like people, so I don't see why I'd like their children."

"That makes sense."

The accumulation and combinations of the smells of
raw and cooked vegetables, meat, and herbs reminded
Virgil of his parents, how much he'd enjoyed watching
them prepare meals for the circus troupe, and the conversations that had livened up the meals. He wanted to find
those things again. Tomorrow, after work, he'd take a
train. He'd get there at the end of dinner, set up under the
big top; they'd greet him with shouts, his parents' friends
would throw themselves on him and lift him off the
ground; the dogs would bark and rub against his legs; the
coffee would be hot and too strong.

Quentin went on, "Even when I was a child, I didn't

like children. I haven't changed my mind. There's something fascist about our obligation to *adore* children. I like certain children. But most are simply not at all the kinds of people you can hang out with."

Virgil liked the score Quentin was playing. He felt like the member of an audience at a blues concert.

"I've always thought children didn't deserve to be children. The adults got a lot more out of it than the children themselves. Children are so serious, so sure of so many things; they'd make great adults."

Virgil smiled at him. He thought about children. He was sorry for them because they were so fragile, so dependent. Their solemnity disturbed him, as did their feeling of responsibility regarding their family and the world, and the high incidence of their suicidal behavior when they crossed the street without looking or swallowed things. But he admired their enthusiasm and their curiosity.

The lasagna recipe had a high fat content. Quentin browned the ingredients in olive oil before adding them to the finely chopped meat, and then Virgil crumbled it into a frying pan. His appetite was coming back.

"So, Clara has moved."

Virgil lowered his head and concentrated on the meat, to hide the expression on his face and his bad-actor smile.

"Yes," said Quentin, "she lives on quai d'Orléans, île Saint-Louis."

"Really?"

"Strange, huh? She's always living in surprising places. She'd had enough of boulevard Pereire, I understand how she feels."

"Is it a big place?"

"Minuscule. She barely has enough space to turn around. But the view of the Seine is beautiful."

Which means she lives alone, thought Virgil.

"Of course, she wasn't able to take all her stuff. Most of it's in my cellar and in our parents'."

Virgil was finally at the point of getting some information about Clara. He felt like a burglar, a Peeping Tom. He had the impression he was committing a sacrilege. It made him uncomfortable. He didn't want to try to find out anything more. Now that he could finally see Clara—all he had to do was wait here, she was arriving in a little more than a half hour—he understood the absurdity of the situation. He didn't want to ask her for an explanation. He didn't want to startle her with his presence, prove how clever he'd been, show that he'd taken his revenge and come out the winner in this story. It was an idiotic victory, and he had no taste for turning the tables. Now that he'd found her, the only thing left to do was to disappear from her life. He'd never been a part of it.

It was Quentin's turn to concentrate on his lasagna. He wanted to ask a question, but was afraid of seeming awkward. He poured the meat into a casserole. It sizzled and gave off steam. Quentin put down his spatula and lit a joint. He offered it to Virgil, who declined.

"Why did she leave you?" he asked, blowing out the smoke. "She didn't talk to me about it. I didn't even know that you were together."

The question caused a pang. He didn't think before answering. He'd never been so sincere. His eyes stung; the vapors from the cooking weren't there for nothing.

"I behaved badly. Toward her and toward myself."

"I never saw you two together. But I know her. And here you are tonight, which tells me that obviously the two of you are a good match."

They were the words of a kitchen mate. We always want those with whom we share an experience as intimate as the preparation of a dish to be close to us. The scent of the marijuana mingled with the smell of lasagna that was coming into being. Virgil took the glass of wine that Quentin held out to him.

"I'd like to start again at zero," said Virgil. "Make it as if we'd never been together."

"That's difficult."

Quentin must have been thinking of his share of romantic disappointments.

"I know. But we can behave as if that's the case."

He fantasized that they met by chance. They saw a Lubitsch at the Quartier latin, exchanged novels, went walking in the Parc Montsouris, had coffee at the Escalier Cajun, dined at Gladines in the Butte-aux-Cailles, then went to the Grande galerie de l'évolution at the Jardin des plantes. The question was knowing how to accomplish this meeting by chance. Virgil would find a way, he knew. As long as Clara didn't take charge of it herself. He finished his glass of wine.

"I changed my cell phone number," he said, holding out a piece of paper. "If you could please give it to her."

"Sure."

Quentin took the paper and put it into a glass jar where he kept his change. He went with Virgil to the door and shook his hand for a long time, as if he were passing on reserves of energy and warmth.

Immediately after having left Quentin's apartment, Virgil, despite fatigue and hunger, felt the desire to take a trip on the Seine by the light of the moon. He had climbed aboard a Bateau-Mouche near pont Saint-Michel. The water and the sky shared the same sad black tint. The thin line of civilization, its constructions, its populations, was squeezed between these two abysses.

The cold was moving in. People had gone out wearing scarves and hats. The red leaves of the trees were like maple syrup candies. Virgil sat down on the deck with a group of tourists. He was holding a cone of hot chestnuts between his two hands. He threw the shells into the river.

An old Chinese couple put a camera in his hands. They wanted Virgil to immortalize this moment. The man and the woman got into position on the edge of the platform, with Notre-Dame in the background. Virgil pushed the button. The flash illuminated a fragment of night for an instant. The Bateau-Mouche passed île de la Cité and headed for île Saint-Louis. The tourists went into raptures before the beauty of the city.

For a long time, Virgil had thought that men and women had to deal with three misunderstandings: meetings, relationships, and separations. You meet, you fall in love, you break up for reasons that aren't clear to you. No couple can escape that set of misunderstandings. It was one of the witty rants he made at dinners and parties. But behind the humor was the sign of his certainty that love didn't work. And like everyone, he was attached to his certainties. Losing them amounted to breaking his arm to give it a different way of bending. For Virgil, relinquishing his pessimistic vision constituted a personal risk that was much greater and more painful than the end of any of his love affairs.

He had no facts, no proof to back it up, unless you counted his inner journey of the last ten days, but he had no doubt that he had no memory of Clara because she incarnated a novelty that went against his beliefs and represented something he could have loved.

The Bateau-Mouche passed under pont Saint-Louis. The tourists were silent. When the boat returned to the light of the moon and the floodlights shining from other boats, they cried out with joy. The boat went past île Saint-Louis. Virgil peeled a chestnut and bit into it.

There's only one way to keep from ever risking losing those whom you could love. It consists of not letting them into your life.

The streetlights on boulevard de Magenta were partly hidden by the trees; their light was reflected back toward the sky by the branches. Virgil treaded on the last leaves of fall. Night had sent men, women, and children on their way; it had stopped the cars and lowered the security gates of the stores.

Virgil had wanted to find Clara so that he could get to know a woman who'd had an amazing and poetic idea. He didn't love her. He didn't even want to love her. It was too early. It was simply the sweet madness of her approach that he liked, and for the moment, that was enough. Maybe she was being facetious; maybe she'd been captivated and had used this surrealistic method to try to attract his attention. In the end, it didn't really matter. By some arrangement of chance, they'd meet one day and would finally get to know each other.

The farther back in time you go in the universe, the more extreme density and temperature become. There is a moment called Planck time, beyond which our physical consciousness will not allow us to go. During the very first moments in the history of the universe, there was no space and time; gravity and relativity did not apply. The meeting with Clara was part of these primordial and unknown moments. Since it happened, Virgil's life had undergone some shake-ups worthy of the birth of a new world. Explosions, collisions, the forming of stars had taken place.

Thanks to Clara, Virgil had learned one thing that he hadn't been aware of until then: he could live. He'd discovered that he was capable of acting and changing and had left behind outdated and pathological notions. From now on, even if his senses told him that the earth was flat and fixed, that it doesn't rotate or revolve around the sun, he knew that the sky was not the limit, that infinity exists, and that our perception of reality supplies us, most of the time, with a false idea of it. As far as humans were concerned—and it was true particularly for the subcategory of love—an axiom could be postulated: what you believe to be, isn't; don't trust appearances; don't limit yourself to convention.

By putting an end to a relationship that had never taken place, Clara had given him an invaluable gift: a story. During the course of these two weeks of adventure, he'd regained his taste for fiction, for the freedom it allows. The missing moment of their encounter would remain present in him forever, like a secret organ that doesn't appear in any anatomy book, but without which the heart can't beat.

Virgil inhaled the cool air of this October night. He was alive. Never had he known it with such intensity.